THE VICTORIAN MILLHOUSE SISTERS

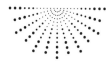

DOLLY PRICE

PUREREAD.COM

CONTENTS

CHAPTER ONE

The settled rain made the afternoon seem very short indeed, and night had settled in before the children were drawn to the window to watch for their father. They heard the factory horns, and knew that within a short time, he would pass the window and knock smartly upon their noses pressed up against the glass, causing them to draw back with glee and then rush to the front door to greet him. Sometimes he dangled a little bag and the children screeched with delight –currant buns! Their wait seemed to be longer than usual today, but that did not put them off their vigil.

A chorus of delight arose as the beloved figure suddenly appeared outside the window, knocking on the glass, and Papa was set upon by three small ones as the door opened, bringing a blast of cold wind into the front room, causing the fire to momentarily blaze up and spark. He took off his coat, hung it on a rack, and swept the youngest, Gabriel, barely toddling, into his arms and to great cheers, held up the brown bag.

"The happiest time of my day, coming home to my wife and children. And the smell of a good supper." he added, kissing Mrs. Swansea, who had come from the kitchen.

"Oh dear, I was a little worried because you were late." said his wife. She was still very much in love with her handsome spouse. They'd known each other since they were children. As a girl she'd idolised him, this fair-haired, good-natured, clever, steady youth, the dream of every mother for her daughter as he found work with the renowned Smithfield Warehouse on Portland Street and was promoted to foreman at the young age of twenty-five, upon his own performance and the reputation of his father before him, who had risen even higher before his sudden death at the age of fifty.

As a girl, Amelia Heaslip thought she hadn't a hope or a prayer of him, but had loved him from afar. She was a poor, ragged, mill child from Manchester's Deansgate, and his family lived in a better part of the area. She'd left the mill and had gone into service at twelve, and had a much better life away from her chaotic home. After she'd been in Havershall Hall for a few years, she had a little money to spend on herself and made herself look nice. Every Sunday she could, she'd gone to her old parish church, St. John's, to admire Charles Swansea from afar. The summer she had turned seventeen she had stayed on for a church picnic. Charles asked if he could sit beside her, and from that time, neither had eyes for anybody else. He had begun to walk all the way to the country to call upon her and take her out, with the permission, of course, of Mrs. Havershall who in general disapproved of *'followers'*, but had taken an interest in Amelia. She'd demanded an introduction, and Mr. Swansea had passed her examination with flying colours.

Amelia and Charles became engaged within three months and married six weeks later. She was the envy of every girl in the parish, and it was murmured that the daughter of Bob Heaslip, a known drunkard, had done astonishingly well for herself. Not so her brother and sister – Sarah had married a man just like her father, and Fred was turning out to be just like him, but unmarried, he lived in doss-houses and drank every penny he made from odd jobs.

Amelia looked up to her husband in every way. He was her life, and though she would not admit it to anybody, she loved him more than she loved her children, and she loved them dearly. He was a good provider, an affectionate husband and father, and her only fear was that, like his father, he would die young. His own kin did not bother much with Amelia; they thought that Charlie had lost his mind to marry a girl from such a family.

The Swanseas lived better than most of their neighbours, many of whom shared their terraced houses with another family, or used their parlour as a room for a lodger. But the Swanseas had their house all to themselves, and the parlour, next to the front room, was a real one, where Mrs. Swansea kept her good china and a silver tea set in a mahogany cabinet. The table was a match for the cabinet. The children were forbidden this room but a fire was lit there at Christmas and if there were visitors expected, like her in-laws when they deigned to visit, or Mrs. Havershall. Mrs. Swansea was proud of having such a good connection, la, not many women who had been in service had their former mistress look out for them as she! Mrs. Swansea kept the parlour spotless, for she felt that if Mrs. Havershall called upon her, she would be offended if the cabinet or the china were not free of dust and had a good shine. Her poor beginnings had made her very alert to the opinion of her betters.

There were three rooms upstairs in their cosy abode. Every bed had a rug beside it so that nobody had to step out onto a cold floor. A scullery and a little garden at the back was theirs. The clothesline flapped with well-kept garments and in summer, bright luxuriant hollyhocks, suggested by Mrs. Havershall, flourished by the fences dividing them from their neighbours. A cast-iron bench sat under the kitchen window, not that Mrs. Swansea had much time for sitting there, unless she was sewing. She was a skilled seamstress, having learned from Mrs. Havershall's own maid.

CHAPTER TWO

T he children had been fed their supper by the time their father came home on this October evening, so Daphne, Becky and Gabriel sat up at the table for their buns, and afterward played on the hearthrug until it was time for bed. Their father lit his pipe and read the paper by the light of an oil lamp. Mrs. Swansea feared gas and would not have it in the house. After the washing up was done (Daphne, aged seven, was old enough to help put dishes away) the two younger children were put to bed and Mrs. Swansea sat with her husband and Daphne, thanking God again that he did not leave her to go to the beerhouse and come home drunk, as her own father had done. No, Charlie was a family man through and through, and did not touch beer or spirits.

Mrs. Swansea hated alcohol and they did not keep any in the house, not even for medicinal reasons. Gas and alcohol were her pet hates.

"Is there any news about Queen Victoria in the paper, dear?" she asked, threading her needle to darn a sock.

"Oh plenty. She and Prince Albert have left for London again."

"It was so nice of them to come and see us as they did; I never thought I'd see the Queen! When she passed us by, she waved. I wonder if she noticed my hat."

"I wonder what Queen Victoria thinks when she waves to people." said Daphne. She was sitting on the hearthrug between them. It was her favourite spot after the young ones had gone to bed, when she had her parents all to herself. She was tracing the design of the carpet with her finger, and her hair, the colour of ripe wheat, fell down each side of her face in thick waves.

"She may be thinking of her dinner, or at least Prince Albert must have been, they'd been out for many hours, looking at the factories and inspecting the newest machines." said her father.

"I'm sure Her Majesty isn't interested in machinery; she has to please 'er husband, you know, for though she is a Queen, she's also a wife." said Mrs. Swansea.

"Becky cried because she wasn't wearing her crown." Daphne said, flicking her hair back. "I had to tell 'er that she didn't tek it everywhere with her, it is so heavy with jewels, isn't it Mamma, and it might be stolen."

Mr. Swansea had moved to another article in the *Guardian*. "Oh, a fire in Sheffield, in a factory."

"Oh don't tell me that, dear. I live in terror of it happening at Smithfields."

"You worry too much, Amelia."

"Mr. Graham took out insurance," Mrs. Swansea said pointedly then, digging her needle into the heel of the sock.

"In case of an accident, that his wife shouldn't be destitute."

"As well he might! Accidents happen in the foundry all the time! No, Amelia, there's no need for me to take out any insurance. There's no danger of it happening at Smithfields. You get too anxious sometimes, and there's no need for that."

"What's insurance?" asked Daphne.

"You're too young to know." said her father.

He rattled the paper. "What did you learn at school today, Daffy?"

"I can spell my name now, Papa. Isn't it enough, and can't I stop now? I want to stay at home now."

"You have to get schooling, Daffy, until you're ten. You'll have a better chance of making a go of your life."

"Your father is right!" cried Mrs. Swansea. "I couldn't go, because I had to go out to work when I was only eight years old. But with your hardworking father, Daphne, you'll be a very fortunate girl indeed."

"Ah! Here is a riddle for you, Daffy. To what eye is everything invisible?"

"I'm sure I don't know, Papa."

"To the eye of a potato." her father answered. "Why is an orchestra of violins like a polite dandy?"

"I don't know, Papa! That's too hard!"

"Because it's full of bows and scrapes. Do you understand?" The little girl shook her head. Her father jumped up, set down the newspaper, and bowed very low to them several times, making them laugh.

"I like that one, I shall remember it!" smiled Mrs. Swansea.

"Another riddle, Papa!"

"No, it's time for your bed now." her mother said.

Daphne sighed, but rose obediently. She felt very grown up being able to sit with her mother and father in the evenings, with her father reading from the newspaper and giving her riddles. It was her favourite time of day. She loved being the eldest child. Becky was two years younger and Gabriel was a baby yet, and neither knew anything. She knew so much more than them. She wrapped her arms about her parents in turn, and kissed them goodnight, and took a candle. She was trusted with candles.

"Take a look at Gabriel." her mother said. Daphne did not have to be told. Her little brother was the darling of her heart. She tiptoed into her parents' room and peered into the cot. He was like a little angel with his curls and his mouth like a rosebud. She wished he could stay a baby forever, and not grow up at all.

Gabriel had been so named because he had looked so beautiful when he was born, and this name had seemed right for a little boy who looked like a cherub in a painting Mrs. Swansea had once seen. And the Archangel Gabriel was a great spirit in heaven, her husband had said.

While not so angelic sometimes when awake, he had a generous nature. Whenever he got a biscuit or even a toy, he seemed anxious to share the joy, even bestowing the bitten biscuit upon whoever was nearby. Mrs. Havershall was charmed by him and accepted his offerings with grace, though nobody had ever seen her finish off the treat.

CHAPTER THREE

Sorrow visited the family in the next year when Grandmamma Heaslip died. She lived with them for a while beforehand, taking the small room at the top of the stairs. She was a sad, wispy woman, and the children did not know her very well before she came to stay with them. While she lived with them, her aunt Sarah visited frequently with their cousins. She was a poor-looking woman; they never visited her house at all – her Mamma could not bear her husband, Ted Bridges. Their cousins wore ill-fitting clothes and no shoes. Daphne wanted to make them welcome but guessed that her mother would not want them coming very often to play. June was her own age and was an amusing, sweet girl, her sister Louisa seemed afraid of everybody she did not know.

Uncle Fred came as well and he always asked for money on his way out again, which annoyed Mamma very much. Uncle Fred dressed badly and had a peculiar smell on his breath that upset her mother beyond anything – her father told her it was whiskey. Sometimes Uncle Fred's eyes looked very strange, like they were sleepy, though he was wide awake. Her mother could not stand having him in the house.

When Mrs. Havershall paid a call to see the dying woman, Mrs. Swansea made sure that none of her other relatives were there that day. Mrs. Havershall praised her care of her poor sick mother, and gave her advice in an undertone, warning her that *'hearing was the last sense to go'* and to be careful of everything that was said in her presence.

Grandmama passed away early the next day. Daphne was glad when the funeral was over; she did not like this business of death at all, with her Mamma crying and knowing that death was forever, or at least until they met again in heaven. Mrs. Havershall attended the funeral service and her mother seemed agitated rather than grateful about it. It was a relief Mrs. Havershall left directly after the service, without meeting the rest of the family. Her mother was delighted she had not stayed.

Daphne began to have a fear of one of her parents dying. But whenever she tried to voice this fear, the words stuck in her throat. She reassured herself that only old people died. But then why did Mrs. Fisher die, leaving six little ones? Or Elijah Browne, who was only a young man, and had *'faded away from consumption'* as her mother put it?

Every Sunday, unless it was raining steadily, scores of Manchester families went for walks outside the city to escape its grey pall and sooty grime. They passed green fields full of cows, barns filled to the brim with hay, and farmyards with hens and chickens and geese. They liked to stop and look at the houses, and if they were thirsty, stopped at Heron's Farm. There, Mrs. Swansea bought drinks of fresh new milk for her children. The little ones loved to see the cow milked.

"Your own children are so rosy-cheeked, ma'am," remarked Mrs. Swansea about a pack of sturdy little ones running about the farmyard.

"Aye, they are that, ma'am. Thank you."

"The city children are not half so healthy, I think. Country air is much better for them. Perhaps someday, we'll move to the country."

"Can we move to that house, Mamma?" Daphne pointed later to a gracious white villa with pink trim, not far from the farmhouse, set in its own copse of trees. It had pillars and a wide porch with a balcony overhead, and bay windows on each side. It was her favourite house in the world.

"When your papa gets rich, Daphne!"

"I'd paint it all pink!" said Daphne.

"Blue for me!" said Becky.

"Dream away, girls!" said their father with good humour.

They saw, in the distance, large homes where the rich people lived well away from the gloom of the streets that housed their factories. Mrs. Swansea always pointed out Havershall Hall, where she had been in service – a gracious three-storey grey stone halfway up a hill, surrounded by a park. But the Havershalls were old money, she said, which Daphne did not really understand.

The question of Grandmamma's death still occupied Daphne's mind and one Sunday, when she and her father were walking alone a little way ahead of the others, she asked:

"Papa, you or Mamma are not going to die, are you?"

"Goodness child, what put that into your head?" her father laughed. "I'm in great health, never better."

Daphne was reassured.

"But what of Mamma?" she persisted.

"Mamma is very healthy too," her father said. "But why are you asking these odd questions?"

She told him. He patted her head and told her not to worry. There was no fear of either of them losing their health, and she could expect them to live until they were very old and plague them until she was grown up.

Daphne was reassured. Her father knew all. If he said so, it must be so! Her handsome, strong father could do everything. He could get a blazing fire going in minutes, fix leaking pipes, clear gutters, shovel coal, paint rooms, carve faces on turnips, and make wooden toys. She was very proud that he worked in that fine warehouse on Portland St, in a building almost as big as Watt's Warehouse, which everybody knew. And he knew all about the government. Last Sunday, on their walk, they had met Mr. Hedges, a schoolmaster, and she heard her father tell him what the Prime Minister should do about the price of corn, and Mr. Hedges was very much in agreement.

"Father," she said suddenly, reassured now that he was healthy and in no danger of dying, "I have an idea. Why don't we move to London, and you could tell the Prime Minister about what he should do about the corn, and advise him in all sorts of other ways. You can tell him about people mocking Manchester and calling it *Cottonopolis*; he mun not know of that, Papa! He can tell Queen Victoria!"

Her father laughed heartily, which she was a little hurt about, but seeing that, he quickly said:

"I'm not laughing at you, Daffy, you have a sensitive soul, bless you. I was laughing at a joke I saw about the Prime Minister, in the paper. Your idea is a very good one, but we can't leave Manchester, for we're Mancunians through and through. As for *Cottonopolis*, is it not something to be proud of, to have over a hundred cotton mills in our great city?"

But Daphne was not satisfied. Important as her father was at Smithfields Warehouse, she felt he could be more important still, helping to run England.

CHAPTER FOUR

"**M**rs Havershall is calling next Thursday!" said her mother one day, after the familiar scented envelope had been delivered by the postman. "La, we have to clean out the cabinet, Daffy, and polish the silver. For she gave it to us, you know, and wouldn't like to see it dull."

"You polished it last week, Amelia," said her husband with only a mild reproof in his voice. "This house is clean enough for any visitor."

"Oh of course it is, dear," she replied, "But I do so want her to know I'm grateful. Only for Mrs. Havershall … " she did not finish the sentence. She felt her husband must be tired of hearing how Mrs. Havershall had given her a chance to better herself when she was eight years old.

Thursday came. Mrs. Havershall's carriage was expected at three o' clock. At five minutes to the hour, there was a knock at the door.

"She is here!" cried Mrs. Swansea, pulling off her apron. "And I never heard the carriage!"

"Mamma, it can't be her, because her carriage is not there," said Becky, looking out the window.

Her mother opened the door and her face fell.

"Freddy!" she said. "What are you doing here?"

"That's not a warm welcome for yer brother, now is it? I 'aven't been 'ere since Mamma died. And you 'aven't been to see me, nor Sarah neither, for that matter. We could be dead for all our sister cares about us."

"It's nice to see you, but you can't come in, not now. I'm expecting a visitor."

"Am I not a visitor, Amelia?"

Daphne saw the scruffy man with the peaked cap, torn jacket and wide trousers in the doorway. It was a long time since she'd seen Uncle Fred, and he looked even worse than she remembered. She knew her mother wanted to be rid of him as soon as she could, but she did not know how it was to be done before Mrs. Havershall arrived.

"Hallo, Daphne, Becky." Freddy took off his cap in expectation of being asked in.

"What do you want?" asked Mrs. Swansea sharply, placing herself in the doorway. "I know it's not to pay me a social call."

"I'm very down on my luck, Amelia. I have no money for food or baccy. Just a few shillins, if you can spare them, would help me greatly."

"I told you never to come here looking for money! Go away, afore you upset me!"

"I'm 'ungry, Amelia. I 'avent eaten all day. Come on, a bit o' bread then. Where's your family feeling?" Daphne thought she heard a desperation in her uncle's voice.

Mrs. Swansea paused.

"Wait there then." she said sharply, and shut the front door in his face. She went quickly back into the kitchen, returning with a cut of loaf bread and some cheese wrapped in a bit of paper. She set it on the table and reached into the jug on the mantelpiece, taking out some change, and thrust the money and bread into her brother's hands.

"There. Now go away, and don't come back. Go quickly."

But it was too late – a carriage had come around the corner and stopped at Number 6.

"Go away," hissed Mrs. Swansea, filled with panic.

Mrs. Havershall, a tall, gaunt lady in a high hat and ermine-lined cloak, was stepping out.

"Your swanky friend." muttered Fred.

"Mrs. Havershall! Welcome!" greeted Mrs. Swansea, with her usual curtsey.

Fred replaced his cap on his head. He set off directly, ambling down the street, unwrapping the loaf as he went.

"A poor old tramp." said Mrs. Swansea, overcome with confusion, hoping that Mrs. Havershall would not remember him from the funeral of two years before.

Daphne felt suddenly ashamed of her mother. That was not nice at all.

Mrs. Havershall was ushered into the parlour. Daphne took her cloak and hung it carefully over a chair, then left to swing the kettle over the fire.

"That was very Christian of you, Amelia." she heard Mrs. Havershall say. "But I would not encourage it. Did you give him money? He will drink it."

Mrs. Swansea's face flamed red.

"I gave him bread also." she said awkwardly.

"If you feed them, you know, they will never look for work. I did not hear him thank you! There is no need to look grieved, Amelia! You surely do not mind my giving you advice! Do you?"

"Oh, no, ma'am. I am glad of it. What you say is true indeed." Mrs. Swansea overcame her embarrassed feelings. Mrs. Havershall had not made the connection between her and her brother.

"You have a kind heart, and I'm just reminding you to use good judgement." Then in a more cheerful voice, she asked, looking about her, "Now, where is Gabriel? Taking a nap, I daresay! I declare I must see how he has grown!"

Daphne brought in the tea, Becky went to fetch her brother and all reverted to normal.

CHAPTER FIVE

D aphne had now been out of school for some months, and was happy at home. She'd hated school. It was boring. She wanted to be home with her mother cooking and sewing and learning everything a girl should learn. But instead most of her day was spent doing housework, as her mother thought she might go into service as a housemaid when she was fourteen.

"But she need not work at all!" said Mr. Swansea, miffed. "Am I not able to keep my daughters until they marry?"

"Of course you are, dear, but Mrs. Havershall has offered to take her –"

"Mrs. Havershall is not the head of this house, Amelia." her father said, gently but firmly.

"Oh, of course not, dear, but she does like to help us, and has given me so many nice things!"

Mr. Swansea rattled his paper.

"I think your gratitude is a bit overdone, Amelia. Your friend hasn't enough to occupy her mind. Don't be led and said by her. Daffy is not going to work, nor Becky. I wasn't going to tell you tonight, but Mr. Smithfield is about to promote me."

"My darling husband! Of course he will!" Mrs. Swansea put down her sewing. Her eyes shone with pride and joy.

"There's one disadvantage, though, I may have to go back to work sometimes after tea. Mr. Smithfield and the Board have decided that repairs to equipment will take place in the evenings, so as not to interfere with the work during the day."

"They'll expect more of your time?" asked his wife.

"I'm afraid that is the case. Amelia, in the future, when I have learned all about the business, I hope to go into partnership with Mr. Byrd, and have our own warehouse. 'Swansea & Byrd'. How does that sound?

"Oh my dear Charles, it sounds perfect. Daphne, your father is going to be a very important man! And Mr. Byrd is such a good man too."

Mr. Byrd was an occasional caller to the house. He was a bachelor about ten years older than their father, was not at all handsome, and was never shown any special attention like being ushered into the parlour, nor would he have expected it. The front room was good enough for him. He was a large, bulky man, with a broad head topped with wiry ginger hair, a red face and long ginger whiskers. He blew his nose with great noise, and slapped his thigh to make a point, and was not anybody Mrs. Swansea would like to introduce to Mrs. Havershall. But he brought sweets for the children, so he was a very popular visitor with Daffy, Becky and Gabriel.

CHAPTER SIX

"**M**amma, teach me how to bake." Daphne begged. Her mother relented, and within weeks she could turn a good cake out of the oven, without a big sag happening in the middle, and produce perfect currant scones. She turned eleven in May 1855, and after that her mother taught her how to sew a whole garment, instead of mending tears and sewing on buttons. She proudly began a shirt for her father's birthday which would be at the end of August.

The week before his birthday, her father announced that he'd have to return to work every evening the following week.

"I have to supervise the men working on the hydraulics, the lifts that bring the stock up and the orders down. It's impossible to do during the day because they are in such demand."

"In the dark, Papa?"

"The warehouse is well-lit with gaslight, Daffy. The better light gets, the more night work will become popular in the future, I think."

On his birthday morning, Daphne presented him with his new shirt. It was of white calico, and she had sewn every stitch with care.

"I will wear it to church on Sunday," he told her. "I'm very proud of you, Daffy! You'll make some man a good wife, but mind you choose well."

"As I did," said Mrs. Swansea, her eyes aglow as usual when she looked at her husband. "She sewed every piece. I only had to help her with the cutting out."

"Mamma is going to bake a cake for you this evening, Papa." Becky announced,

"Shhh! That's a secret!" Daphne said.

It was a happy gathering that evening for tea, but her father had to leave shortly after they had their cake. He kissed them all goodbye. After the washing-up was done, Mrs. Swansea took her place by the hearth, her sewing on her lap. Daphne was knitting. Mrs. Havershall had declared that it was a good, useful activity, and she would encourage every girl to learn it. She herself had seen a most exquisite baby gown at the Great Exhibition; it was said to have over a million stitches. The metal needles clicked. Yes, it was a good pastime, and it was nice to see the solid square grow larger as she worked the needles. This was just a practice piece but perhaps she could knit a pretty shawl for Mamma, if Mrs. Havershall could guide her. Becky was practicing stitches on an old handkerchief and Gabriel was playing on the hearthrug with his little wooden horse and donkey, making them race each other from the row of blue diamonds on one side to the red diamonds on the other, jumping them over the stripes between.

"Why does the donkey win all the time?" Daphne asked with humour. "It's not fair on poor Wellington, is it?"

"Wellington is letting Neddy win, because he knows he'll get a bag of oats from Neddy's master." said Gabriel, galloping the donkey once again toward the finish line ahead of the horse.

"And who might that be?"

"It's Mr. Smithfield! Didn't I tell you that yesterday, Daffy?"

They all laughed. None of them had ever met the owner of Smithfield Warehouse, except their father of course, who whenever he was summoned to speak to him, or even happened to glimpse him, told them of it with awe. He was a god-like figure, with wealth and power and mystique.

Time went by; Father should be home soon, Daphne thought. Becky and Gabriel went to bed, Daphne usually waited up with her mother. It was past ten; where was Papa?

Mrs. Swansea was becoming concerned. She put away her sewing and made tea. Perhaps he would come when she was brewing it. But she poured; still no sign of Charles. They drank their tea and washed the cups.

At eleven, she was very worried, and at half-past eleven, she opened the door and looked up and down the street. All was dark and quiet, except for a couple of men coming home from a pub.

"Have you seen Mr. Swansea?" she called out to them. They looked at one another and came over.

"No, Missus." They halted, a little uncertainly, Daphne thought. She had followed her mother outside.

"He's always home by now." her mother continued. "He works late sometimes. At Smithfield Warehouse on Portland Street. He's senior overseer there." she added, though the last sentence was irrelevant; it was routine now on her part to add it whenever she mentioned where her husband worked.

"There's a fire somewhere around Portland Street," one of the men said. "Maybe he's delayed because of that."

"A fire! No, not a fire! Oh I hope it's not at Smithfields!" she cried out. Daphne felt anxiety rise within her.

"You have to go and find out, Mamma!"

But her mother would not go, not even when a peculiar orange glow began to light the skies over the chimney tops, in the direction of Portland Street. News of the fire began to spread, lights were lit as people got up and went into the street to see the glow. Younger people dressed themselves hastily and took off for Portland Street to see it up close.

"Father mun have stayed to help the firemen put it out," said Daphne. "Mamma – look – the Quinn girls are going, I'm going with them. Ellen! Mary! Wait for me!"

"Tell Papa to come home directly!" cried her mother as Daphne ran back to get her shawl and then took off after her neighbours.

CHAPTER SEVEN

The Quinns were all agog to see a fire, but when they heard that Daphne's father worked on Portland Street, and was working that very night, they had the grace to dampen their excitement. As they neared the area, they were joined by surging crowds - Manchester had awakened and was coming to see the spectacle. Even if no lives were lost, a disaster at any of the mills or warehouses caused great anxiety for those who depended upon them for a living. Men could be turned out while repairs were made and stock replaced, sometimes for months on end, and hunger could strike many a family.

Drawing into the streets nearer Portland, it became apparent to the crowd that this was no minor fire, as flames and sparks shot over eerily-lit chimney tops.

"What's on fire?" asked Ellen Quinn of a bystander, as they finally came to Portland Street.

"Smithfields Warehouse. It's nearly gone."

"Are there people in there?"

The man could not say.

Seeing the stout, solid building attacked by raging flames, taller than any Daphne could even imagine, caused her to cry out:

"Where's my father? He was working tonight!"

Her words caused people around her to startle, and the word quickly went around that there was the daughter of a man who had been working this night and could yet be inside. People turned to look at her, and a path was quickly made for her to advance. The Quinns pushed through to stay close by her. Ellen was about sixteen and knew what to do.

"We should find a fireman," she said, and ran over, past a police barrier, to one of the men training a hose on the building, ignoring the angry objection from a constable. The fireman shouted something, and a man in a top hat and greatcoat, his necktie askew as if hastily arranged on his way out his front door, made his way to Daphne, who had been thrust to the front of the crowd.

'It's Mr. Smithfield.' went the murmur among the people near her.

"Who are you, Miss?"

"I'm Daphne Swansea! Mr. Charles Swansea is my father!" cried Daphne. "He was working tonight! Where is he?"

But the man made no reply, only looked grimly at the devouring flames.

A scream rent the crowd as two figures were seen at a second floor window. Daphne looked up. More cries went through the gathered people. *A sheet– quickly–a sheet!* One was quickly procured, and within a few minutes several men stood under the window holding the outspread linen taut. By now the crowd could see the figures were a man and a youth. They appeared to struggle with each other. Then the older forced the younger out the window, and he fell onto the outstretched sheet. A sudden flame spurting from another window illuminated the man who was left inside, so that for an instant, he was clearly visible.

"Papa!" screamed Daphne. "It's Papa!" The man appeared not to hear her above the roar of the fire and the loud panic of the throng. He fell back, coughing, out of sight. A ladder to the window was quickly erected, and a brave fireman scaled it in moments, but as the flames shot out the window, he was forced to descend.

"Papa! Papa! No, Papa!" Daphne fell to the ground amidst the thick boots all about her.

CHAPTER EIGHT

"**A**melia, please eat something." Sarah stood over her sister, a bowl of soup in her hand. "You can't stay like this forever. You 'ave to get up and look after your chillun. They need you."

"He shoulda saved himself. Why did he do it? Why?"

"Because Jem Fountain is a lad of fourteen!"

"You keep sayin' that! Better a child to die than the father of a family! He should have thought of us! I hate him for it, I do."

"You're not the only broken-hearted widow, you know. There's twenty-four others. And others burned, that'll never work again. Are they all carryin' on like you are? I bet they're not. They're up carin' for their chillun."

"He had a chance to be saved – and he din't take it!"

Daphne was listening at the top of the stairs. Her mother's words sent a chill through her. She could not hate her father, who everybody was calling a hero. What he had done was even printed in the papers, even in the London papers. She crept downstairs again.

"We're not going to get much money from the Relief Fund they began. Only the labouring families will get it – jus' cos my husband was senior overseer, they think we're well off and don' need it!"

It had been four weeks. Four weeks of pain, grief, and horror. They had found Charles Swansea's charred remains. Her mother had not left her bed. She had not been able to go to the funeral. Aunt Sarah had taken Daphne and Becky to the service and to the churchyard. They had never really known Aunt Sarah before this, and she was a very good, kind person. She was looking after them like a mother and their cousins were a comfort.

Daphne carried the last glimpse of her father in her mind all the time, that harrowing sight of him at the window, his face cut up with despair. She'd never seen him like that, ever – it shattered her image of him – her strong, loving father, able to do everything, and equal to any situation! She'd told Aunt Sarah about it. Her aunt had said that her Papa went unconscious as he fell back, and wouldn't have felt the flames. Daphne believed her. She wanted to.

Mr. Smithfield had paid them a call, together with his secretary, who bore a month's wages with him. Daphne had remembered to open the parlour for this important person, though there was no fire, and she served them tea there, which at first they declined to have, but then seeing that this young girl wanted to do something for them, agreed.

Old Mrs. Swansea and her family were steeped in grief and shock. They had come to see Amelia, but neither party had been any consolation to the other, Amelia had complained bitterly about his refusal to take out insurance. Charles' mother and sisters were in no mood to hear their fallen loved one treated so, and took their leave very rapidly, refusing tea.

The only action that Mrs. Swansea had thought of taking was to immediately send word to Mrs. Havershall. But that lady was visiting friends in the Peak District, as she did every autumn, and was not expected back for some weeks.

There was a knock at the door – more visitors to pay their sympathies, no doubt. Becky answered as Daphne sped downstairs.

There was a women there some years older than her mother, her head enveloped in a shawl.

"You don't know me," said the woman. "I'm Mrs. Fountain, Jem's mother. I wanted to pay my respects – I shoulda come afore now, but Jem couldn't be left – he was burned on his arm and neck, but he's recovering. I'd be without my Jem if it hadn't been for Mr. Swansea!"

"You have to do something for yourself!" Aunt Sarah's frustrated cry came from upstairs. She must not have heard the knock. It was becoming a refrain heard at all hours of the day. She knew her mother's answer – same as always – "I want to die!" Clearly heard below.

"I'm afeard Mamma isn't up to receiving visitors yet," Daphne said lamely, her face red. "She's taken it very hard."

"I understand. I'll come back 'nother time," said the woman. "Poor dear! Don't say I have bin, 'her if it would upset her more – I know 'ow she mun feel!"

No sooner had Mrs. Fountain left, than the rentman came. Of course, the rent was due - overdue. She took the money from the jar on the shelf and paid it. Her father's wages were being depleted very rapidly. And with no father now, how were they to pay rent next month? And the next? Their lives had been turned upside down.

She was about to shut the door when this time, a team of horses cantered down the street, followed by the familiar carriage that halted at their door. Mrs. Havershall was back! At last, there was hope. If anybody could get her mother out of bed, it was Mrs. Havershall. She opened the door wide even before the lady got out of the carriage, and greeted her warmly ushering her upstairs, introducing her to Aunt Sarah, then hurried to get her a chair so that she could be seated at the bedside.

Mrs. Swansea wept afresh when she saw Mrs. Havershall, made a half-hearted effort to sit up in bed, and fell back among the pillows again.

"We are ruined, ma'am! Completely ruined! My husband dead! He 'ad no insurance, and we are going to be destitute! I can't stand it!" Her mother cried out loudly, tossing and turning in her bed, flinging the bedclothes off of herself in her agitation. "I can't bear it! I can't! I will die!"

Mrs. Havershall shook her head.

"It is a dreadful business, Amelia. You have my deepest sympathy." She turned to address Daphne. "Is there any brandy in the house?" she asked.

Daphne did not know what brandy was. "Oh no, Ma'am. But I will make you a cup of tea."

"Goodness, child! Not for me! For her! She needs a dose of something. Here." Mrs. Havershall opened her reticule and took out a silver coin." Go and give that to Begley. Tell him to go to the nearest tavern and buy a bottle of good cognac. Will you remember that? *Co-nyack*."

Daphne obeyed, repeating the word to herself as she found the coachman outside, who was laughing with Ella Quinn. Daphne felt very awkward interrupting them – they were happy, happy in a world where only a few yards away there was utter heartbreak. How odd it was, that in one place, people laughed, and just a little bit away, others had broken hearts!

But they became serious as Daphne approached with her errand. Begley knew exactly what *co-nyak* was. He jumped up on the box without delay and set off.

Within a short time, a bottle of amber liquid was in Mrs. Havershall's hands. She asked for a small glass and poured a quantity in.

"Now, Amelia," she said in an authoritative voice. "You are to sit up and drink this. I will not take no for an answer."

"If you please, ma'am, she always said she never wanted to drink, not a drop." Aunt Sarah said, a little forcefully. Daphne looked at her, a little concerned. Why was Sarah opposing Mrs. Havershall? Would it not do her mother good?

"Nonsense! This is medicinal! Come on, Amelia."

"I don't want it," said Mrs. Swansea, shaking her head wildly from side to side as the glass approached her lips. It was the first time she had opposed her patron. "No, no, not that. I hate even the sight of it! And the smell! I beg you, don't make me drink that!"

But the more she opposed Mrs. Havershall, the more forceful the lady became.

"Daphne, help me. Go to the other side of the bed, climb up behind her, hold her head - like so. She shall have it. She shall. Open your mouth, Amelia!"

"It's scalding me!" screamed Mrs. Swansea, as a stream poured past her lips and into her mouth.

"That's just because you are not used to it. It only scalds for a brief moment. Come on, Amelia, another sip." Mrs. Havershall drained the glass into Mrs. Swansea's mouth. The woman coughed, her face grew bright red, and then she settled back upon the pillows, her chest heaving as she complained again of burning, this time in her chest.

But she became calm and fell asleep within minutes.

"You see, it has helped her greatly. I will leave the bottle with her, and you are to give her more, Sarah, later, when she becomes restless. Poor soul! Such a sensitive, frightened little mouse she was when she came to me! Always anxious to please me and everybody around her. I like to think I have done her good in her life, but as to what is to happen to her now, nobody knows, still – something must be done. I shall not abandon her." Mrs. Havershall took her reticule and stood up to leave.

"I will return tomorrow." she said.

CHAPTER NINE

Mrs. Swansea had another drink of brandy that evening. Aunt Sarah locked the bottle away for the night. Mrs. Havershall gave her another drink the following day. By then, she had accepted that the drink was not as bad as she feared – it was helping her. She got up and dressed herself.

The children were very happy to see their mother up and about again, preparing a meal. Aunt Sarah and the cousins returned home. Mrs. Havershall called one more time, telling Mrs. Swansea that she had a good plan for the future – Daphne was to come to her house when she turned twelve, and she would train her as she had trained her mother before her. Mrs. Swansea was not to allow her nerves to get the better of her.

That evening, a poor fire burned in the hearth. Gabriel played listlessly with Wellington and Neddy. Mrs. Swansea took up her sewing, and set it down again.

"I need a bit more of that brandy," she said. "Go and get it out of the cabinet, Daffy."

Daphne obeyed. Her mother took a long draught. "There isn't much left," she said anxiously. "Has my brother Fred been here, helping himself to it?"

"No, Mamma. Is that whiskey, then?"

"No, but it's very like."

"Mamma, Aunt Sarah didn't want you to take it."

"I don't want to take it either, but – it's no harm, for a little while, until I begin to forget. It helps me to forget."

"If it helps, can I have some? There are things I want to forget." The image of her father's despairing face rose again in front of her.

"Gracious no, child! It's not for children! It ruined my father, and has ruined Fred. I shall have no more, when this is finished. No more. We shall carry on as best we can."

CHAPTER TEN

Two days later, Mrs. Swansea left the house for the first time since her husband's death. She returned with groceries and began to cook. Daphne was very relieved – her mother was coming back to herself. The children missed their father acutely, the sound of the factory horns in the evening reminded them of Papa, and the sight of neighbouring men coming home from work stung their hearts as they saw other children greeting their fathers at the doors. Daphne began to take Gabriel under her wing, to take him places with her, to teach him his letters, for it was high time he began to learn. He should begin school soon. Becky gave up school. Daphne was aghast, but her mother said school was not necessary.

"I've come to a decision, girls. Daphne, you are to go to Mrs. Havershall as soon as you turn twelve, and as for you, Becky -"

"What will I do, Mamma?"

"You can work in Coopers Textiles, where I worked a long time ago, and where I intend to return to work. You'll get a bit of schooling there, it won't be all work. That's the law now."

"Mamma, she's only nine!"

"I'm only nine!" Becky repeated, wailing. "Why can't I go to Mrs. Havershall as well?"

"You're too young to work in her house, I was eight when I began to work, and no schooling! You shall go, Becky. We'll need your wage as well as mine! The rent here mun be paid, for I won't move out of this house, and go to some horrid little place. How could I, with Mrs. Havershall my patron?"

"But Mamma, you always said that you were too young to work, at eight years old!" Daphne protested. "Becky is only a year older!"

"Yes, Mamma! I want to go to school! My friends are at school!"

Their mother began to tremble. "To have my own children oppose me, after all I have suffered, is a cross I can hardly bear!" She got up and went upstairs.

"Will they beat me at Coopers?" wailed Becky. "I don't want to go!"

"Shhh! Don't let Mamma hear you cry; it will make her angry. Don't worry, we shall think of something, we will."

"Why did Papa die?" Gabriel asked miserably. "I want my Papa!"

Daphne took him on her lap and comforted him as he sobbed.

CHAPTER ELEVEN

Mrs. Swansea got a job at Coopers Textiles, and took Becky with her. They went out before six in the morning and returned extremely tired at nine that night. Mrs. Swansea's job was operating machinery all day long. Becky's was in another room with the looms. Sometimes the threads got entangled underneath the machinery and only little bodies could squirm under them and only small fingers could work them free. A team of little boys and girls swarmed about wherever there were tasks that could be done only by little ones.

When they got home, Mrs. Swansea went straight upstairs; she did not want any supper. Becky fell asleep over her bowl of broth and bread, and Daphne had to wake her to go to bed, and she was too tired to undress herself, so Daphne had to put her to bed as if she were a baby.

The job lasted only three weeks. Mrs. Swansea slept late several times, making her and her daughter late. They were sacked. Becky was very happy about it, Mrs. Swansea had developed a kind of numb expression on her face, so Daphne could not tell her feelings.

One Friday in November when the rentman called, Daphne went to the jar to take out money. But she shook out only a few pennies.

Her mother was in the kitchen.

"Mamma? The rentman is here and the money's gone!"

"I'm sure I don't know how that happened, Daffy."

"But what shall I tell him?"

"Tell him to come back next Monday. We'll have it for him then."

Mr. Jones was not pleased. He lectured that Mr. Grayson, who owned the street of houses, would not brook any delay, and that if the rent wasn't forthcoming on Monday, then they were out on the street.

"Mamma, I don't understand where that money went," said Daphne. "And where are we to get money enough for Monday?"

"I don't know," said her mother, and she said it almost as if she hardly cared. Daphne left the kitchen for the front room, and shovelled some coal on the fire, but sparingly. Perhaps Mamma could ask Mrs. Havershall if she could begin work before she turned twelve next May – yes, she could begin next week perhaps – and Mrs. Havershall could advance her wages to pay rent. But they would have to go to Havershall Hall tomorrow to ask her. She could take her belongings with her tomorrow, in the expectation of being taken on there and then. She got up quickly and went to the kitchen to tell her mother her idea, excited that it would work. Opening the door, she saw her mother drink from a small bottle and put it away in the cupboard.

"What do you want?" asked her mother, roughly.

"Mamma, what was that?"

"What?"

"What were you drinking?"

"Medicine," said her mother, before seating herself at the table, her head in her hands.

Daphne went to the cupboard and opened it. She took out a bottle labelled ' OLD TOM GIN.'

She knew it was a spirit. She put it back, then left the room, thought for a few moments, and went upstairs to her mother's bedroom. Searching, she found a box of empty bottles under her bed.

That was why they had no money now. Her mother was spending it all on gin. She did not know what to do about it. She was horrified, and knew that she could not handle this herself. She resolved to go and see her Aunt Sarah, who would advise her.

CHAPTER TWELVE

Daphne donned her shawl and made her way over to Blossom Meadow. She did not come here very often, to the place where her mother's relatives lived. It was a long walk, and the district was poor, dirty and very run-down, full of horrid sights and smells. Barefoot children shivered on doorsteps. Scrawny dogs fought over a bone. She passed a boneyard and a rough doss-house where a group of scruffy youths jeered her as she went by them. She hurried her steps. At last she found her aunt's small flat on East Street. Aunt Sarah cleared a space for her to sit down on the raggedy couch, and listened with sympathy, her lips tight.

"I'll come back with you," she said. "I was afeared this would 'appen! That stuff is a curse on our kin! She has to give it up, or you'll all be ruined."

Mrs. Swansea agreed that she would give it up, but she had one more bottle to use, and after that was gone, there would be no more. Ever.

Daphne believed her. But Aunt Sarah did not. She demanded that her sister pour the bottle down the drain, with her watching. This her mother would not do.

"You are to find it, and dispose of it." Sarah instructed Daphne out of her mother's hearing.

"It's not in the cupboard. It's not in her bedroom. I don't know where she keeps it now," Daphne said. "We'll be evicted on Monday. I don't know where we'll go."

"Oh goodness, Daffy. Pawn something! The silver, or the china – that'll get you enough rent money and groceries too!"

"But Mamma would never allow that!"

"Then you 'ave to do it behind 'er back. I 'ave an idea. Go and get something now from the parlour, while she's upstairs. Go get the silver jug. We'll go to the pawnshop together and see what we get for it. It might be enough for the rent and groceries to tide you over. And don't tell 'er what you did."

Sometime later, Daphne returned to the house with two pounds, and some bread, tea, sugar, milk, jam, herrings and bacon. Her mother never asked her where she got the money, though she looked at her with great suspicion.

Daphne hated the position forced upon her, that of outwitting her mother in order to keep food on the table and a roof over their heads. Her mother soon found what had happened, and Daphne only feared that she'd take the other valuables now and pawn them, but keep the money to spend on gin.

The rent was paid on Monday, but after that, Daphne found the parlour locked and the key not in the dresser drawer where it had always been. She was in despair. Her mother was going out and buying the foodstuffs they needed – and gin. She drank upstairs, stayed up late pacing her room, stayed in bed late, and got up around midday. Her appearance deteriorated. She did not bother to do her hair, and clothes went unwashed and unmended. It was nearly Christmas and Daphne asked her for money to do some shopping. She entered the parlour for the first time, to see the mahogany cabinet almost denuded of the china and the silver, those objects that had been her mother's pride and joy. Daphne wept. The extent of her mother's decline was glaringly evident. What was she to do?

Then one day, two men came and took away the cabinet and the table. Mrs. Swansea kept the money she got for them. For the next few weeks, they ate very well indeed, almost like old times. Mrs. Swansea began to do herself up respectably, the rent was paid and the children began to be happier again.

Mr. Byrd called during this time and as it was nearly dinner time, was persuaded to stay and partake of the roast beef and Yorkshire pudding. He had left Smithfields and was now with a smaller company, Webster Cotton, he said, where he expected to be eventually named as a junior partner. Mr. Webster was a good, fair man, he said, slapping his thigh.

"That was a very good dinner, madam," he said, before he left. "My landlady, unfortunately, is a mediocre cook."

Money began to be scarce again not long after that, and there was no more good food. Aunt Sarah urged her sister to move to a smaller house or take in a lodger – they were paying rent for rooms they weren't using! But Amelia would not consider it. She began to go out at night, and Daphne put her little brother to bed. She was supposed to go to bed herself at nine o'clock, but one night, waited up in the dark. Her mother came in at eleven, parted from somebody at the door – a man! Surely not a man!

"Mamma!"

"Daffy? You were supposed to go to bed." she sounded angry, and her speech was slurred.

After that, her mother seemed to have a simmering anger, but not saying anything at all.

"Mother, talk to me, please!" pleaded Daphne one day.

"I'm as bad as my father was." said Mrs. Swansea.

"Don't say that, Mamma! You can get out of this – all is not lost! When I go to work, I'll send money home! I want to begin as soon as I can. Mrs. Havershall is coming to see us very soon"

"Don't mention that witch!"

Daphne felt as if she had been hit.

"Mamma, Mrs. Havershall is our friend."

"She is no friend! Who is to blame for me bein' like this? Not your father. Not you, not Sarah, but Mrs. Havershall!"

Daphne was dumbstruck. Was this really her mother who spoke? Her world was changing very quickly indeed.

Thursday arrived. Where was Mrs. Havershall to sit? They could say that there was no fire in the parlour; yes, that would be a good excuse, and they would seat her in Papa's old chair by the fire, the best one in the house.

"Mother, are you not going to do your hair?" asked Becky as three o'clock neared.

"I'm sure I'm good enough to meet anybody," said Mrs. Swansea with bitterness. She wore an old patched gown and a dirty apron.

The carriage was heard, the rap on the door came – Daphne opened it. Mrs. Havershall swept in.

"We have no fire in the parlour," Daphne said awkwardly, indicating her father's old seat by the hearth.

"And that is very sensible of you. I would not like it lit just for me. How are you, Amelia?" she looked curiously at Mrs. Swansea, who was seated in the chair opposite.

"I am as you see me."

"Oh come now, Amelia, you must pull yourself together. For your sake and for the sake of your children. Why Gabriel, you have grown! You will be a handsome lad someday! Do you know, Amelia, I have very interesting news – my coachman Begley is to marry, and you will be surprised when I tell you who it is!"

"Who?" asked Mrs. Swansea.

"It's Miss Ellen Quinn, your neighbour! Romance has blossomed while I have been paying my visits here! Is that not something!"

"She should stay single if she 'as any sense." said Mrs. Swansea.

"Oh now, Amelia! What kind of talk is that?"

"It's just what I mean."

Daphne had swung the kettle over the flames to boil water for tea.

Mrs. Swansea rose and went upstairs. Mrs. Havershall's eyes followed her. Then she turned her questioning eyes to Daphne.

"I have to tell you, Mrs. Havershall," whispered Daphne. "Mother is in trouble. She – she drinks! She's spending all our money on gin, and Aunt Sarah 'as been over, and tried to talk her out of it."

"Good Heavens! This will not do! I will talk with her! She will ruin you all, you'll be in the workhouse before you know it! No, she must stop this!"

"Stop what?" Mrs. Swansea said, coming down the stairs.

"Daphne told me you were drinking gin. You must stop, Amelia!"

"Oh I know I am. And who got me started on it, eh? Who?"

"What – who are you speaking of?"

"You know full well! It was you! You forced that brandy down my throat! I begged you not to! You did it! Only for you, I'd be orright! It runs in the family and I feared if I started I would never stop! Like my father! My brother Frederick, who you met one day at the front door and took for a tramp!"

Mrs. Havershall had risen from the chair, her face white.

"Amelia, I did not mean to – you were moribund upstairs – I was merely trying to help – I was ..."

"Mamma doesn't mean a word of what she's saying!" interrupted Daphne. "She'll be sorry the minute you go out the door!"

"I must leave this moment! I will not stay here any longer!" Mrs. Havershall took up her cloak and swung it about her shoulders.

"Mrs. Havershall – when can I begin work with you? Please, I will go with you this very minute – we're that desperate - "sobbed Daphne, clutching her cloak as she swept toward the door.

"You will not go, Daphne! Never!" cried her mother, pulling her back, as Mrs. Havershall made for her cloak.

Becky watched from the window. The coachman was retrieved from Quinns. He hopped up on the box, flicked the reins and with the clatter of hooves upon the cobbles Mrs. Havershall disappeared from their lives.

"You made an exhibition of yourself, Daphne! Begging, like that! As if you couldn't bear to be 'ere with your own family! You're a disgrace to me!" Mrs. Swansea took to her room again, and Daphne sobbed by the fire, her spirit almost broken. Becky rushed to comfort her. Gabriel went out. Only five, he already found that being out on the streets was more peaceful than being at home. He would go and hang around Mrs. Turpin's door, who would take pity on this waif, whose mother was too sotted on gin to look after her own children, and bring him in for bread and jam. The neighbours had forgotten already the tragedy that had befallen the Swanseas – they saw only that the widow was known at the gin palace on Kettle Street, and that they'd soon be on the Parish, all of them.

CHAPTER THIRTEEN

C hristmas came and went, no cheer, no presents, no hot chocolate, no bonbons, no decorations, and no cheery blaze in the hearth. They shivered while eating a meagre dinner of rabbit stew and potatoes. And all missed the presence that had always made Christmas a happy time for all – their beloved father. Mrs. Swansea's anger had burned itself out and she began to truly mourn him, for he had made her very happy and had been a wonderful father. He was a hero, a fine man!

"We have no rent money, Mamma."

"We can sell one of the beds."

"We'll only have one left!"

"So? We can all sleep in one bed."

Daphne felt the injustice, the great disorder in their lives. Gabriel was a beggar going about the neighbourhood – that she knew. She took off once again for Blossom Meadow, and her aunt had only one solution. Amelia had to move to a lesser house, and she knew of a vacant place just around the corner. She marched Daphne to the landlord, and Daphne returned home with the news that they were to move, without having seen the place. Her mother made no objection. Aunt Sarah knew a man with a cart who came and removed all of their belongings the following Friday, and they left the only house they had ever known, for a dank space in one of Manchester's worst slum districts.

They looked about them in silence as they entered. It was only two rooms, front and back! This place was worse than Aunt Sarah's. But Uncle Ted worked, even if intermittently, in between drinking bouts. The back room – a scullery – had foetid water running down the walls. Daphne pulled Gabriel from there when he darted in because he saw a rat. The scullery was unusable, and the stench unbearable.

"How are we to live here, Daphne?" cried Becky in anger, while their mother just sat numbly on a chair.

"To have come to this." she said unhappily, very quietly, while the men brought in the few pieces of furniture they had left.

Their one bed was set up by the wall, a wardrobe placed beside it, and their table and chairs set in the middle of the room. That was all. They paid the men and sent them away, then unpacked their boxes. It did not take long – nearly everything had been sold or pawned, but Mrs. Swansea had kept a few of hers and the girls' best clothes. She'd sold her husband's, only keeping a few items to make clothes for Gabriel.

"I will take in sewing," she said. Daphne said nothing. She had already tried this, and had not delivered the items on time, so that she had lost the job.

Daphne put the clock on the mantelpiece, and arranged some ornaments around it. Mrs. Swansea made a fire in the grate.

It spluttered and blew smoke back into the room, so that they coughed.

"Mamma," said Gabriel. "When we go to heaven, we'll have a nicer house, won't we? I'll be very good!"

"Oh yes, darling, you will be very good I'm sure, but you mun pray for your poor Mamma."

Daphne felt sick in her heart. It tore her inside that her mother was so helpless in the face of her craving for gin. She loved her, and sometimes she wished that she could take the burden from her.

"Mamma, I'm hungry, I am." Gabriel complained a few minutes later.

Daphne took a few coins and went out to look for a shop. She felt that they had landed on Manchester's scrapheap. It was even hard to breathe here. She felt coal dust settle on her face. Becky and Gabriel had gone to a water pipe that Aunt Sarah had told them of. They returned to the house all together. The fire was out. There was no sign of their mother, so Daphne set their meal of bread, herrings and water on the table and they ate hungrily. Where was Mamma getting the money for gin? She truly did not know.

Mamma did not return until early morning. By then the three children were in bed. Becky and Gabriel had fallen asleep but Daphne was awake, miserable. There were cries and shouts from everywhere about. Two men fought loudly outside the door. Would they fall against the door and would the lock hold? Babies cried. A dog growled on and off. There was some laughter – but who could laugh in this place? The rare moments of quiet were interrupted by scuttling in the corners of the room. She dropped off to sleep eventually, but dreamt of being on the street, in the middle of the fight, unable to pass. She did not hear her mother come in and join her three children in bed.

Winter wore on. Spring was very welcome, though the warmer weather brought its own problems. Daphne and Becky joined Aunt Sarah, and their cousins, at their place of work, the Maltings Factory. There, they endured the long hours and drudgery of sweeping and keeping machinery clean. Their mother 'took in sewing' as she had intended to do, but the work was rarely completed or not done on time, or became soiled because she fell asleep and it dropped from her lap to the floor, so she lost clients as fast as she made them.

Becky blamed Mrs. Havershall for all their misfortune, but Daphne knew that her mother had to bear some blame also.

CHAPTER FOURTEEN

I t was a hot week in July. Gabriel was running a fever. They had all become sick on and off since they had moved. But now a dreaded disease was sweeping Blossom Meadow like a broom gathering everything in its path, sparing nobody it touched. Cholera!

When the girls returned from work that evening, Gabriel was listless, weak and pale. Mrs. Swansea was trying to give him sips of water.

"We have to get a doctor, Mamma! Becky, you and I will go for the doctor. You will stay here with him, Mamma?"

"Of course I will." her mother replied, with an indignant anger.

The doctor was out on calls, so they left a message with his wife. Gabriel's condition deteriorated rapidly. He could not drink or eat, and they were having to change him like an infant at frequent intervals, for cholera gives the stomach no rest.

They watched, helpless with horror, as he slipped away from them.

"Gabey, Gabey – you have to stay with us. Don't go!" his mother wept in great grief. "I'm sorry, my darling child. Oh is this my fault?" she wept again.

He was beyond any earthly help, and died in her arms.

He was buried in the Pauper's Cemetery. Their mother seemed to be in such grave shock that she did not eat for days. Nor did she go out, and Daphne searched the room for drink secreted somewhere, without finding any.

Had her mother been cured of this curse, at last? Had it taken Gabriel's death to bring her to give up drinking?

"Oh God, may it be so." she prayed.

A few days later, her mother, sitting with them late at night, said: "Girls, I have come to my senses at last. Your remark to me, Daphne, as to whether I would stay with Gabey while you and Becky went for the doctor, hurt me deeply. It showed me what you thought of me. Am I really that bad in your eyes, Daffy? If I am, I only have myself to blame. I don't know if Gabey would have lived if I had stayed in every night, nevertheless, I feel guilty about his death too." She began to sob.

The girls went to her and embraced her. They all cried. She recovered herself after a few minutes.

"And I've made up my mind about something very important. I'm going to get us out of this present situation. I have an idea. Daphne, Becky – we have sewing to do."

CHAPTER FIFTEEN

F rancis Webster, owner of Webster Cotton, took one look at the invoice that had come in the morning post and rang the bell. Their servant, Kitty, was in his study a moment later.

"Is Mr. Ethan still here?"

"Yes, sir, he's not gone out yet. Shall I send 'im up?"

"Directly, please."

A few minutes later his tall, grown son opened the door of his study.

"What is it, sir?" he asked sulkily.

"It is this!" He threw the bill at him. Ethan picked it up as if he had never seen one before in his life, and read it.

"Would you like to explain yourself?"

"It was like this, sir. As you know, my friends are very well off. Lord Longstone, for instance, and Hobbett-Smith. You do not want your son looking like the poorest gentleman in Manchester, do you? They all order from Chaucer Square or

Bond Street, sir. You haven't seen my new hat, sir, and when you do, I think you'll agree it was worth every penny."

The door opened and Mr. Webster groaned. The Campaigners had arrived — the boy's mother and his two sisters — no doubt they had listened at the door.

Three pairs of eyes reproached him.

"Papa, dear, don't be cross!" Helena simpered at her father.

"Papa, he has to look as well as his friends!" Lavinia's expression was one of annoyance.

"Dear husband, please remember that our family has to keep up a good appearance!"

Ethan basked in their assistance. His countenance looked relaxed, even smug. His father's expression darkened in displeasure.

"I can do nothing against all of you lined up against me, it seems. Very well, go and spend all the money you want in Town, young man. And see your mother and sisters destitute after I am gone."

"Oh, Papa, you are too cruel!" squealed Helena, the younger.

"Ethan shall marry money, if we are strapped for money," was Lavinia's opinion. She had no intention of marriage, and being the eldest of the family, ran her brother and sister's lives as much as she could.

"There's no fear of destitution, never you mind." soothed the maternal voice.

"Whatever you say. I sha'nt care either way, in my grave."

"Come on girls, your father is out of spirits this morning," Mrs. Webster ushered her daughters, ages twenty-four and seventeen, out of the study. Ethan made to follow them.

"Not so fast, young man."

"Yes, sir?"

"I don't expect the women to have much appreciation of where money comes from, for they simply spend it. But you, my son, have to know the value of honest work. Longstone and Hobbety-Hobbety or whatever his name is may be gentlemen, and may drive their barouches about all day if they please, but you will find an occupation. You're twenty-one years old and need to settle to work. Tomorrow, you accompany me to the Mill and there you will apply yourself, all your days, from now on, that is, if you expect to inherit."

"Yes, sir," Ethan sulked again. He left the room and banged the door.

CHAPTER SIXTEEN

E than sat at a desk the following morning, sulkily examining long books of accounts. It was still three hours to dinner-time and he was already bored. His father was at his desk just feet away, likewise absorbed in figures, when Mr. Byrd came in with a question for him. This needed some discussion, so he drew up a chair and together they examined some books.

The door opened and the clerk came in.

"There's a *lady* to see Mr. Byrd, sir." he said.

A female person in the offices! Ethan looked up. This was a matter for distraction. Perhaps he'd find an excuse to go out and take a view of her.

Byrd looked astonished at the news, which Mr. Webster found amusing. This confirmed bachelor had a lady coming to see him, what was afoot? His mother and sister were far away in the West Country from where he came.

"Did – did she say what her name was?" stammered Byrd.

"She's a Mrs. Swansea, and she has her daughter with her," said the clerk.

"If you will excuse me –" Byrd said with confusion, his face turning an even deeper shade of red. "She is the widow of Charles Swansea, who died in the Smithfield fire, if you remember."

"I do remember! Well, there then, take as much time as you wish." said Mr. Webster, still amused.

Mr. Byrd emerged from the office to see Mrs. Swansea and Daphne, attired in mourning dresses of black poplin, seated on a couch which was there specifically for visitors, only usually they were businessmen, buyers and bankers.

"Mrs. Swansea! To what do I owe this pleasure?" the man said, acutely conscious that the clerk was listening. Curse that Higgins! Would he not absent himself?

Mr. Byrd had always admired Mrs. Swansea, her pretty, pert eyes and her sweet, helpless manner. He liked seeing how she used to defer to her husband.

"Oh Mr. Byrd, I must speak with you! You know our circumstances are greatly altered since – "she looked down at the floorboards and took out her handkerchief.

Higgins was not taking the hint, so Mr. Byrd beckoned to them to come into a back office, a small space hardly bigger than a cupboard, where mother and daughter were seated on the only two chairs. Mrs. Swansea's crinoline practically took up the entire space. Mr. Byrd shut the door.

"We've had such sorrow this past year," Mrs. Swansea went on. "We had to move, you know, to an area of Manchester far less appealing than Deansgate. And Gabriel, my little boy became ill – he is no longer with us."

"Oh, I am so sorry to hear that!" Mr. Byrd burst out. Daphne saw something in his eyes as he gazed upon her mother. Something more than sympathy. Was it – admiration? Did Mamma know that this man loved her?

Mrs. Swansea talked for another few minutes about losing Gabriel.

"I am sorry you suffered such trouble, and I was not aware of it. I would 'ave done something for you, if I would have known. Is there anything I can do for you now?" he asked, with a clumsy tenderness.

Mrs. Swansea paused.

"There is one thing, perhaps. Daphne was to go into service with Mrs. Havershall – you know, of Havershall Hall." Mr. Byrd had never heard of the place, but he nodded anyway.

"Mrs. Havershall is in a position in which she is unable to keep her promise." Mrs. Swansea looked down.

"I would not have my daughter take a position in any house without knowing the character of the family," she went on. "So if you would be so good as to use your influence with Mr. Webster to ask his wife if there is any vacancy in his household for a parlour maid. Daphne is an excellent seamstress, cook and housekeeper."

"Say no more, Madam," he said with a brusque tenderness. "It is a sad situation you have come to. I will do what I can."

"So altered! Everything so altered! We are come to this, to have to go into service! Her father never wanted that for her! But what choice do we have now? I work as a seamstress, but I want to get Daphne settled in a good situation soon."

"You must work, Mrs. Swansea?"

"Indeed, yes. My husband never took out any insurance, and Smithfields as you know, did not pay compensation, on account of his being blamed for the gas explosion that night …"

Daphne looked at her mother in amazement. This was news indeed! Was it true?

"Most unjust, Madam. I will do whatever I can, I promise you."

"I knew you would, Mr. Byrd! My husband always said you were the most honourable, the finest man he knew! And I know, from those brief visits you made when he was alive – in much happier days - that he spoke the truth."

Daphne had never known that Mr. Byrd had been held in such high esteem by her mother. But she saw Mr. Byrd's face flush and a broad smile expose a row of crooked teeth.

"May I have the honour of calling upon you soon?" he asked.

"You are always welcome, Mr. Byrd. I would like so much to invite you to sup with us, but our fare is so simple now, and our accommodation reduced to just one small room, in – Blossom Meadow, of all places, that I can't offer my visitors anything but the most basic refreshment. Now, do you think badly of us?"

"Blossom Meadow! As bad as that?"

"He left me in terrible debt. Everything we had is gone to repay the debts owed to – unscrupulous people — ruthless, unscrupulous people. I shall say no more." She dabbed her eyes with her handkerchief.

Daphne looked in astonishment at her mother.

"Charlie in debt!! Dear Mrs. Swansea, why did you not come to me afore this? But I could never think badly of you, Mrs.

Swansea, no matter where you were lodged!" he said. "I just wish to call upon you to see what I can do for you."

"We would be so grateful for anything, Mr. Byrd. We are quite desperate!"

As Daphne and her mother emerged from the office, she saw a tall, lean young man cross in front of her. He gave both of them an interested, though impertinent look.

"Mamma," said Daphne, as they walked back home. "I think Mr. Byrd is in love with you!"

"He always liked me. I could tell."

"But – are you in love with him?"

"No, not at all."

"Oh, Mamma. Are you going to break 'is heart?"

"Oh, not at all!"

"I din't know you were suggesting me for Webster's, it's a good idea, Mamma."

"Daffy, mark my words, you shall never be in service at Webster's."

Daphne was so astounded she could not say another word on their way home, except to ask her mother if what she had said about her father being blamed for the fire, was true.

"Unfortunately, yes. They had to blame someone, you know. But I know it was the gas."

Daphne was upset that her father, who had given his life for another, had been blamed by his bosses for the fire.

"But what of the debts, Mamma? You never told us of any debts."

"There were none. But I had to explain Blossom Meadow. Your father would not mind I had said that, he only wanted the best for us, ever."

Daphne wondered that if Mr. Byrd knew the truth, would he be as willing to help them?

CHAPTER SEVENTEEN

As soon as Mr. Byrd had been to Blossom Meadow, and walked along its putrid streets and saw the ragged people watching him from doorsteps, and then their squalid, dark, stinking room, he insisted on moving the family to better accommodations, to a small but clean flat near his accommodation in Trafford, *'for the sake of the friendship he'd had with Charles,'* he had said. He paid the rent and gave Mrs. Swansea money to live on, again *'for Charles' sake.'* He came for supper there often, and the girls knew they should take a walk after supper, leaving the couple alone. They were tranquil – their mother had given up drinking completely. She was particular about her appearance, she became comely again, and was good humoured.

Mrs. Swansea became Mrs. Byrd on Daphne's thirteenth birthday the following May. They moved to a nice house Mr. Byrd had bought near Crumpsall. The girls were overjoyed. This house on Darlington Avenue was even better than their first house! It was set in its own little garden and had a gate and a fence around it. There were two stories and a big parlour downstairs, and Mrs. Byrd set about furnishing that and the rest of the house. She consulted Mr. Byrd before she made a purchase, and he was pleased at her good sense and economy.

They even had two servants, a maid and a man. This was wealth indeed!

Mr. Byrd liked a glass of port in the evenings, but his wife resolutely stayed away from it. After the summer, Daphne and Becky were sent away to school, as their learning had been very scant. They were sent to Hightrees School for Girls as boarders, and looked forward to letters from their mother, which they received at least once a week, and returned home for Christmas.

"Mr. and Mrs. Webster have invited us for dinner on the Saturday after Christmas," Mr. Byrd said. "Is that acceptable to you, my love?" He beamed at his wife.

"Of course, Daniel. That will be very nice. Girls, you've not met them – but they paid a call here soon after we were married. They came all the way from Victoria Park! What a splendid Park it must be, all new housing, and they have the best neighbours!"

"It was just a short visit, Amelia, and they did not see you blooming as you are now!"

Their mother and stepfather caught each other's eye. Mamma coloured a little, giggling, while Papa – they had been told to call him Papa – looked about him with a big smile upon his face.

"Shhh!" she said to him.

"They do love each other, don't they?" Becky said that evening as the girls prepared for bed. "She's made Mr. Byrd a happy man! And as for Mamma, I've not heard her laugh so much in years. Oh Daffy, aren't we so very lucky now?"

"Everything is good now."

"Good now! The way you said that means that you don't think it will be good forever, and I think it will. What can you mean?" Becky snuggled under the sheet and drew it and the counterpane over her head.

Daphne lay down on her pillow.

"I don't mean that something bad will happen. It's just that – I don't trust being happy anymore."

"Are you afraid Mr. Byrd will die too?" came the muffled voice from under the coverings.

"I don't know what it is I'm afeard of, Becky. I just know that you can think everything is fine, and then something horrible can happen to spoil your life."

"Oh shut up!"

"I do wish we'd go to church again. We always did when Papa was alive. I hope we go on Christmas Day."

"Mamma doesn't believe anymore and Mr. Byrd never believed at all. I 'eard him say so."

"You see, that isn't right. They don't believe in God! No good can come of that. I believe in God, don't you?"

"I don't know. Just because we go to church at school, doesn't mean we have to at 'ome. I'm going to sleep, Daffy. You can be sad all you like, but I'm happy."

CHAPTER EIGHTEEN

Their parents consented to church on Christmas Day, and Daphne loved being there, singing carols and listening to the readings about the birth of Jesus, and meeting people afterwards, neighbours that she had never seen before. They had a fine dinner later on. Mother and daughters remembered the dinner of last year at Deansgate and how poor and cold they were, how joyless! But little Gabriel had been with them! They missed him greatly, his wide eyes and sweet nature. They had gifts also – dolls for both, though they were a bit grown for them, their mother decided that she had never been able to afford dolls as beautiful and grand, with exquisite clothes she had sewn herself.

The Webster home was new and imposing. 'Larger than Havershall Hall,' whispered their mother as they were ushered inside by the butler. "Behave yourselves, girls, no elbows on the table, and sit up straight. And try to remember your aitches, and don't say *afore* for *before*."

The girls were very polite and pleasant. They were introduced to the family – young Mr. Webster, Miss Lavinia

Webster and Miss Helena Webster. Daffy recognised young Mr. Webster as the man who had looked rather rudely at her mother and herself at the mill. He was good looking but she did not like his stuck-up air. But were they not all rude? They hardly spoke to their visitors. Daphne and Becky were seated opposite them and they merely made conversation among themselves. Old Mr. Webster, however, was very friendly and they warmed to him. After the women withdrew, Daphne was asked by Miss Webster if she could play the piano. She shook her head. Could she recite for them? No. At that, Miss Webster began to play. They overheard Mrs. Webster tell their mother that it was a shame she did not take a little white wine for her health, it was a wonderful tonic, warmed with cinnamon and spices. The girls felt a little alarmed to hear this, and hoped that their mother would not listen to the advice.

"I do not know why you refuse wine all the time, Amelia." said their stepfather as they drove home. "It's a little odd to keep on refusing it."

"It doesn't agree with me, Daniel."

"Very well my dear. I shan't press you."

"Shall we tell the girls our secret, Daniel?" she asked on their last morning at home, at breakfast. They would leave within the hour for Hightrees School.

"Tell us what?" asked Becky, spreading jam on her hot toast. What joy it was to have good things to eat! Her mother had set plates of poached egg, sausage and kippers before her and Daffy.

"You are to have a new baby brother or sister." beamed their mother.

There was great excitement. Their stepfather looked very happy indeed.

"When, Mamma?" asked Daffy, quickly swallowing a bite of a soft white roll in her hurry to find out.

"In early summer."

"Will we be here?" asked Daphne then, with eagerness.

"No, you will not, for you need schooling." said their stepfather with authority.

"Oh Daniel, I would so like for them to be here –"

"Amelia, their education has been much neglected. And you will wish them to marry well, won't you? Remember what we talked of."

"Your Papa is right." sighed Mamma. "You, Daffy, need an accomplishment, and we've decided on drawing for you. For you, Becky, you can begin piano as you have a good singing voice to go with it, and you've wanted to, I know!"

The girls were very pleased. They were also learning to speak better, for they had come up in the world since their mother had married Mr. Byrd.

CHAPTER NINETEEN

S pring passed – it was May. Letters flew to Hightree from Mrs. Byrd's pen, and more flowed back. She was well, and on a bright sunny day a baby boy arrived at the Byrd's house and was given the name Daniel, like his proud father.

Daphne and Becky were wild with excitement and joy at Hightree School when a telegram arrived, and their classmates rejoiced with them. They wrote happy letters home. But their happiness was short lived. Their stepfather appeared two days later to take them home. He and his wife were in the deepest grief – the little boy had died.

"It's not fair," sobbed Daphne. "It's so not fair! I wanted a little brother so much!"

Their stepfather was struck silent with grief. He did not even ask them about school, or French, music, or drawing, or anything that had interested him before. They did not know what to say to him. It was a dreadful blow.

After nine days, Mrs. Byrd got up and joined them for meals. It was a very quiet table. The girls felt a great uneasiness, yet they could not name it. Every meal after that was the same. Everybody was miserable. The clergyman and his wife were turned away by their mother when they called to sympathise. Daphne thought that was very rude.

With no church to attend on Sunday, Daphne felt aimless. Becky kept asking how God could allow this. She didn't believe in God either, so there! She was going to forget all Papa had taught them as children. None of it was real.

Daphne was too sad to argue, and she did not have any answers.

CHAPTER TWENTY

The girls stayed the entire summer, spending most of it with their mother, who could barely allow them out of her sight and did not want them to return to school. During this time Mr. Byrd, thinking that his wife needed something to occupy her mind after her children were back at school, set her to examining his household accounts, and gave her financial responsibilities. Amelia sat in the study every day, wrote notes to banks and offices and visited the bank to manage the Byrd family fortunes, which was rapidly growing as her husband's responsibilities with Webster Cotton grew.

It was early September, and the house was empty and quiet, except for the servant who had long ago finished her dusting and polishing and was in the kitchen. Amelia was in the study, as usual at her books. But she could not concentrate. She missed her girls acutely. Her heart ached for them, and for the child she had just lost, and Gabriel, and her darling Charlie, who had been the love of her life. She felt empty and sad and there was a great yawning space within her, and nothing, or nobody, present to fill it.

Her eyes wandered to the cabinet where Mr. Byrd kept his bottle of port.

Surely a little would not do her any harm? Just – a little?

No, Amelia, don't.

But just once – to get her over this horrible time, just today. A little, a very little, one half of a port glass – no more.

She got up. Why did she feel watched? Who was watching? Were the books lining the walls watching her? The desk, the chairs, the portrait of Mr. Byrd's parents on the wall? *Don't be silly, Amelia. Nobody's watching you.*

She turned the key in the cabinet, opened the door, saw the bottle and took it out, and then reached for a glass from the shelf above. The cap made such a sudden noise as she twisted it off, that it almost frightened her. Don't be silly, she told herself. You're an adult, you're in command of yourself. The wine liquid tumbled into the glass. It was willing! Very willing to be drunk! Everything was in favour of her having this tipple. Half a glass would not do her any good. She'd fill it. She threw back her head and drank.

She wanted another glass, but Daniel might miss it, though the bottle was dark-coloured. Better not take any more though. She went back to her figures but again, she could not bear the quietness. She paced the room. Then she went for a walk about the garden. She brought the glass with her to rinse it in a little fountain. Mrs. Grady mightn't understand if she left it for her to wash. She dried it with her handkerchief and replaced it on the shelf.

The following day the same thing happened. The silence. The tragic memories. The unbearable loneliness. This time she went to the back of the cabinet and found an unopened bottle of Old Tom Gin. It seemed to be waiting for her! She guessed it was a gift from somebody from some years ago, and Daniel had no interest in gin, so she might as well use that. Using a glass complicated things, so she drank from the bottle, and set it by her as she worked on her figures.

She emptied the bottle on the third day. She'd have to replace it – not that he'd miss it – but she would feel uneasy if there was none there. It was just to have there in case she needed it, the very thought of having a bottle there was enough to calm her. She need not drink it at all. But how to get it? There was, she knew, a gin palace three streets away. She was not known there. What if she took a walk? Walking was good for her. And better not to keep it in the cabinet after all. She did not want Daniel to find out, because he might misunderstand the situation. She'd keep it in a drawer of her dressing table, under lock and key of course, and she'd keep the key on her person.

Amelia, isn't this like what you were doing before? Remember how it ruined you, and your family? murmured an inner voice.

Nonsense! She answered. *That was completely different. This time, I am in command. I can't ruin us, because Daniel has a great deal of money. Besides, who are you to tell me what to do? Go away.* She shut the voice off.

CHAPTER TWENTY-ONE

Christmas came, and Mrs. Byrd had a fear that her daughters would find out what she was doing, but they did not suspect, as she drank lavender water to give her breath a nice scent. Her husband had no suspicions. But he had to work some nights now, and Mr. Webster sent him to London, Liverpool and Exeter sometimes for a few days, for the company was expanding, and young Mr. Webster was unreliable – a bad lot, Mr. Byrd called him, not at all like his father, but showing every sign of turning out bad. A wastrel!

Daniel's absences exacerbated her loneliness, and at night, she often walked down the street, hailed a hackney and was taken to the gin palace, the Golden Grove.

Not only was she a regular at the Grove, but she'd met a man there – a friendly, charming man named Richard Montague. It was an innocent friendship – at first. He amused her and made her forget her troubles. He liked to gamble; loved the horses. He encouraged her to try her hand, took money for her to put on a bet, and she won ten pounds the first night.

In time, their friendship became more intense. Montague was often down on his luck. One day, he'd get the Big Win and retire. She began to lend him money.

"I'll pay you back," he promised, "When I get the Big Win. I feel it can't be far away."

She continued to keep the household accounts, and Mr. Byrd never looked at them. But he did like how wine agreed with her now, for she always joined him in a drink, and it never seemed to do her any digestive harm. He and Amelia had gotten over their great disappointment, and both were happy. Just one thing was amiss – he always took the post with him in the mornings, and she was not writing to the girls as often as she should, which was odd for a mother. He had mentioned it once but she had become upset and said that she missed them so much it made her sad to write, which puzzled him very much.

Another strange thing was that Mrs. Webster had, upon passing the house one evening when she was on her way home from a friend's house, decided to pay her a call, because she knew that Mr. Byrd was away. But the maid had said she was not in. Where had she been? Amelia had seemed a bit confused, and Daniel did not know if she was quite herself.

CHAPTER TWENTY-TWO

"**A**melia, I have been keeping a surprise for you," said Mr. Byrd one evening after he had come home from work. "Last week, Mr. Webster called me into the office and made me a junior partner!"

"Oh Daniel, that's wonderful news. I knew you had it in you!"

"And that's not all, dear wife. We're moving to Victoria Park! As it happens, there is a vacant house there, and I already made the offer!"

Mr. Byrd did not see the odd tremble in his wife's hand as she began to rearrange flowers in a vase.

"But I'm very happy here, Daniel. Really, I'd rather not move."

"Nonsense, wife. We must move. We'll have to entertain and keep our own carriage and all that. The other men in businesses will have to visit me. Wheeling and dealing."

"I see – very well – it is … "

"What's the matter? I thought womenfolk loved bigger establishments."

"Nothing, dear, I'm just overwhelmed at the news. Will I be able to manage a houseful of servants, do you think?"

"Oh, I see. That's your fear. We're as good as anybody else, Amelia, though we're rough and ready. We'll go higher than your Mrs. Havisham or whatever her name is! Of course you will manage. Now join me in a glass of champagne to celebrate our luck! Amelia, you can expect the girls to make cracking-good marriages! Wouldn't Charlie be pleased? We'll visit the bank tomorrow to arrange funds for the house purchase – no, Friday – I won't have time tomorrow." He popped the bottle and the champagne sparkled its way into two glasses.

"Here's to the future!" he said, raising his glass.

"To the future!" she joined him, and downed the liquid, shaking like a leaf.

CHAPTER TWENTY-THREE

"**D**affy! Daffy! We're to go to Mrs. Wilbur's room!"

"Why? Is there something the matter?"

Their stepfather was with the headmistress. He looked as if he had not slept for a long time, his cravat was undone, and his suit crumpled, his face haggard.

"Has your mother been in touch with you?" he asked, abruptly. "Tell the truth!"

"No! What's the matter?"

"Where's Mamma? Is she ill?"

"She's not ill. She's gone."

Daphne and Becky were stricken with fear.

"What happened?" cried Daphne.

"She's made off, that's what happened. With another man."

Mrs. Wilbur gasped.

"You will need to take them away directly," she said quickly. "I will have a servant collect their belongings." She pulled a bell.

The girls were husseled into the waiting carriage, and waited ten minutes until their belongings were thrown in there too. They were frightened. Their stepfather paced about outside until they were ready to leave, and then he got in and slammed the door.

"What do you know about this?" he asked.

"Nothing! We've not heard from Mamma for a month at least."

The carriage made its way to the station.

"I have never met such an evil woman in all my life," said Mr. Byrd then, in a savage way that frightened them even more. They moved closer to each other. He was looking at them as if he hated them. The girls clutched each other, too frightened to speak. He had a fiery look in his eyes and they trembled.

"She took me in all right, for everything. She's ruined me. Ruined me!" He held his head in his hands. His fingers burrowed into his wiry ginger mop.

"I have no money left - not a penny. Instead, I have debts! Gambling, drinking!"

Daphne allowed a cry to escape from her lips.

"You knew!" he accused her, his eyes filled with anger.

"I didn't know! I thought she had given it up for good!"

"You mean this happened before?"

"After Papa died – Mrs. Havershall forced her to drink cognac, and that was the beginning of it! She could not stop! She drank gin. Finally, after Gabriel died, she stopped. She swore she would never touch another drop and I believed her!" Daphne was crying now, and Becky burst out:

"It was all Mrs. Havershall's fault, Papa!"

"Don't you ever call me Papa again," he said fiercely. "And stop that loud crying, Daffy!" he paused, looking out the window. "How I wish I'd never paid that call to Blossom Meadow! She never loved me – she used me. You all did. I should've left you there in the dirt."

"You said she was gone off with a man. That can't be true." Becky said. "Mamma isn't as bad as that."

"Well I have news for you, Miss Becky. She is as bad as all that. She's a – " He stopped himself in time.

"Can't you see we are just as angry as you are?" shouted Becky. "Can't you see we are just as hurt, and in a situation now where even if we had all the French in the world, and could play as well as Handel, we are ruined too?"

Mr. Byrd sat back and sighed, looking at his hands. He slapped them on this thighs.

"What is to become of us?" asked Daphne, in tears. "We have no father, no mother, and you are abandoning us also."

He seemed to calm himself. The reminder of their situation, and the great sorrow they were also in, seemed to return him to the man they had known before.

"This is the situation," he said. "I'm not going to abandon you."

They looked at him with relief.

"But we are going to have to sell the house, and move to a very, very small place."

"We've had to do this before," Becky said stoutly. "We can do it again."

"As long as it isn't Blossom Meadow," added Daphne, between sobs. The hurt her mother had caused her was burning her heart like hot coals, and she could not stop crying. But Mr. Byrd was not being horrid now. He was their only hope! They had no provider – except him!

"Not Blossom Meadow." he said quietly.

CHAPTER TWENTY-FOUR

The full story came out in bits and pieces. When Mr. Byrd had returned from work the day after telling his wife about his promotion, she had vanished. No note, nothing. He'd been dreadfully worried and thought she had been abducted, until Mrs. Grady had told him that in the morning, she had been summoned and given an unexpected day off and told to go home.

Her departure had been intentional, then?

But Mrs. Grady had a great deal more to tell him. What the neighbours were telling her. Mrs. Byrd was drinking and gambling.

Where was she getting the money for all this? He had gone to his study and for the first time in two years, opened his books. What he found there caused him to stand and stare out the window for a long time, trying to understand why the sky was still there, and the road, and the trees, and people passing by, when his world was gone. He was utterly ruined. He found unpaid bills and angry demands from creditors and – worst of all, found in her dressing table drawer, tied in a pink ribbon, was a bundle of love letters from a man named *Dick M*. He'd broken down then and cried. The betrayal shattered him. He had gone to Hightrees to vent his rage on her daughters, but when their distress had become apparent to him, he could not but feel for them also. He would not abandon them, but they would have to earn their living.

CHAPTER TWENTY-FIVE

I t was humiliating for him to have to ask the Websters' for help, but they would have to know his altered circumstances. Mr. Webster in particular felt his friend's disgrace keenly. They discussed it among themselves.

"Will you have to drop him?" Mrs. Webster asked.

Mr. Webster shook his head. "He's the best man I have. He stays Junior Partner, since our own son is not up to it. What will become of Ethan, Honoria?"

"He's just sowing his wild oats," said his wife, but a sadness came over her. "He should be settled of course. Oh, if I could only see him married before I ... " She stopped.

"Don't speak of it, Honoria. You are overly pessimistic."

"We have to face the real situation, John. But, back to Ethan. He should get married."

"But nobody will have him. Every mother and father for miles around have warned their daughters off our lazy, dissipated son."

"He is not as bad as all that." the reply was low, and unconvincing.

The door opened.

"Madam, the doctor is here." Kitty quietly announced.

Honoria got up; she was unsteady.

He caught her hand.

"Would you like me to come with you?"

"No, dear. I don't want you to see me – I want you to remember me the way I used to be."

"As you wish, but I want you to know you are very brave, Honoria." He kissed her hand with deep affection and she left to climb the stairs to her chamber, to have her wound dressed by the doctor.

He allowed himself a tear or two. Honoria had breast cancer, and there was no cure. She had submitted to a brutal operation two months ago, and had been growing weaker since then. The illness had brought them closer than they had been for years, and they had recovered a tenderness that had slipped away from them a long time ago.

CHAPTER TWENTY-SIX

Daphne and Becky moved with Mr. Byrd to a very modest house in Cheetham Hill. The girls set about making it homey. There had been a big sale of all Mr. Byrd's possessions and they had kept only necessary items. He admired their bravery. They'd been in this situation before and were accepting of it.

"Where are we to work?" asked Daphne, as they prepared for bed. "There's nothing we can do, is there, that I can think of, that would bring us in a good wage!"

They found out the next day. Mr. Webster had found places for them in his mill. This was not an occupation they looked forward to. Becky had never forgotten her horrible experience at the age of nine.

Daphne had not taken much notice of her surroundings on her visit to Webster Cotton with her mother several years before; now she saw its size. There was a piece of open ground, called a croft, and several buildings surrounded it. Nor had she remembered the deafening noise of the steam engines. Mr. Byrd left them at the door, giving their charge over to a girl called Nan, who led them up two flights of stairs to the spinning room. It was a hot, noisy room, there were fresh grease-stains on the floor and it stank of oil.

"These are the Swansea sisters," Nan said to the overseer, and left them. He was a man about forty years old, grumpy, greasy and tired, even at this early hour.

"Get to the mules!"

The girls had grown up knowing that mules were massive machines used in textile mills for spinning.

"Ye be piecers!" he roared again. "You – " he pushed Daphne toward the machinery, now beginning to make a noise like a train on it tracks "- keep th'ends up!"

Daphne did not know what he meant.

"Show 'er, Tom!" he roared, and a young boy, about eleven years old, took her away.

"You!" he said to Becky. "You sweep floor, under machines an' all."

Becky was terrified of the machines. Daphne could see the overseer shouting at her, over the sounds of the mules.

"I want to run," she said tearfully to Daphne when she had a chance to talk to her some hours later.

"I do too," Daffy said. "Mr. Byrd must've told them that I could piece. I don't know what I'm doing and I've been shouted at all morning!"

"It's unbearable, Daffy, it's unbearable!" Becky was angry.

"Don't do anything silly," Daffy said, truly frightened that her sister would run away as she threatened.

That night, the girls fell into bed. Though very fatigued, Daphne still could hear the sound of the machinery in her head. It pounded and pounded. Eventually, sleep came upon her, but it seemed like only a moment later she had to get up again.

Becky argued with her stepfather.

"What are you doing to find Mamma?" she demanded.

"Nothing. I don't want her back."

"She's your wife! You must try!"

"Don't give me any grief, girl. Or I'll throw you out on the street." Her stepfather had lost any sympathy he had for the girls. Now he felt burdened.

"I'm not staying here for much longer." Becky said darkly to her sister some weeks later as they walked to work. "I'm going to go and look for Mamma, if he won't. Will you come, Daffy?"

"No! You'll be looking for a needle in a haystack, Becky."

"I can't stand the Whisker." It was their nickname for their stepfather.

"You two never stop sparring. But what will you do, Becky?"

"I don't know. I'll see." They had reached the mill and the sounds of machinery was getting louder.

"I'll find work somewhere in the outdoors – selling vegetables or ribbons – something like that. I'll be a servant, anything. Anything but in a noisy, smelly, oily mill."

"You're only fourteen, Becky!"

"Don't tell the Whisker, or else I won't tell you when I'm going. I'll just disappear after dinner someday, with nothing, no clothes nor food, nothing."

"All right, Becky! I won't stand in your way. Just be careful"

Becky decided to go early one Sunday morning. Daphne still agonised about telling their stepfather. What if something happened to Becky? She was too young to be on the streets, making her own way! But she knew that when Becky wanted to do something, she did it.

"Who knows when we'll see each other again?" she said, crying in their room as Becky donned her cloak and picked up a bundle of belongings.

"We'll meet again. I'll write if I get news of Mamma," Becky promised. She stole downstairs and went out the door, closing it very quietly.

Mr. Byrd slept on. Daphne decided to get up. She would go to church! She dressed and hurried out, and sat at the back of St. Matthew's, her head down lest anybody see her tears. The words and hymns were comforting. A dreaded task lay before her – that of telling Mr. Byrd that Becky had left. He was more annoyed than worried – "I expect she will find her mother – that's all right then, and maybe you can join them both when she is found. By the by, you'd best call me Father or Papa again, it's not respectable for us to be under the same roof and you calling me Mr. Byrd."

CHAPTER TWENTY-SEVEN

Becky Swansea left her stepfather's house with great hopes. The streets on Sundays were quiet, an alteration from the bustle of every other morning in the week, when they were filled with people hastening to work in the dawn mist, their clogs hitting the pavement, coughs muffled inside cravats and shawls.

She had no money, but she had food wrapped in a cloth – a half loaf and some cheese and cold beef. She would get water at any pump or pipe. Her belongings were in a bundle easily carried over her shoulder.

She was determined in her plan, and having no fear, or any regard for propriety, thought nothing of going into any pub, tavern or beerhouse in search of her mother. She was determined.

She turned her steps towards Crumpsall, and stood outside the house they had lived in on Darlington Avenue. How happy they had been there, her and Daffy! Now there was another family living there.

But where had her mother drank? The Golden something. Golden Globe? Glove? Grove? It was a few streets away in the direction of an old stable, near a railway arch. It was probably closed on Sundays though. There were families walking the streets, coming from church. Oh the silly people, didn't they realise God wasn't real? If He was, why didn't he prevent tragedy, like what had happened to them?

Becky wandered about and found the Golden Grove a few streets off.

The door was closed and the windows were shuttered, but there were people inside, she could tell, from a chink she peered through. She knocked on the door, and getting no reply, knocked on the window.

"What do you want?" a man snapped at the front door. "We're closed, and you're too young to be coming in here. What age are you, fourteen?"

"I'm sixteen," lied Becky, "and I'm looking for someone who might know my Ma."

"Who's yer Ma, then?"

"She's Mrs. Byrd, Amelia Byrd, and she lived on Darlington Avenue. She used to come here, and she's gone missing. She went off with a – another person - and I know she must've met him here."

Becky was not shy and never beat about the bush. The man's eyebrows raised.

"Come in," he said, with a jerk of his head.

It was dark inside apart from the light of a small lamp. A little collection of people were gathered there, eating and drinking. A few women looked at her curiously. She looked back at them, boldly. What were they staring at?

"She's lookin' for 'er Ma." The proprietor jerked his thumb at her.

"It ain't me," chuckled a woman with wispy blonde hair and a glass in her hand.

"What's yer ma's name, Miss?" said the other woman there, examining her closely.

"Byrd. Amelia Byrd."

"Oh, Amelia!" said the first one. "We knowed Amelia!"

"Did you?" Becky sounded eager. See, how easy it would be to trace her mother! She'd find her in no time, and bring her back, no matter what the Whisker would have to say.

"Where is she?"

"Well I don't know, do I? She went off with Dick Montague, din't she? He used to hang around those places in Tupper Square."

"Where did you live, Miss Byrd?" asked the first woman.

"My name is Swansea, actually. My mother remarried after my father died."

"Where did you live? Around here, was it?"

"On Darlington Avenue."

"Some nice houses there," said a man, turning around and looking at her curiously. "What number was it?"

"Number 10."

"And – where do you live now?"

"Nowhere, as of this morning."

"Say, Miss, I can do you a big favour if you can do me one." he said.

"What's that?"

"I will help you find Montague, and yer ma, if you can describe Number 10 to me, how if there are any windows at the back that are not easily overlooked by other 'ouses, for instance."

Becky looked at him in confusion, before it dawned on her what was being asked.

"Shut yer mouth, Jack." said one of the women crossly.

Jack turned his back and resumed his beer.

"Where should I look in Tupper Square?" asked Becky.

"In a place called The Blue Bird. It's a doss-'ouse. The manager, Pug Grainger, has a room out back where people play cards, and that's where Montague used to go. And yer ma too."

Becky made her exit. Tupper Square was a few miles away. Just a little walk. She got hungry when she smelled dinner from the houses she was passing and stopped to eat her food. She reached Tupper Square in the afternoon and saw the Blue Bird Lodging House. What a run- down place! The walls were peeling paint and the windows were hung with dirty lace. She rapped on the door. A man opened it and asked her what she wanted. The smell of greasy food drifted from the interior and she heard the hum of conversation.

She repeated what she had said before. But this man frowned.

"Yer not looking for lodging, then?" He sounded threatening.

"No – well … " an idea occurred to her. "I might be, yes, I am. I need a place to stay tonight. And I will need supper. Do you serve food here?"

The man laughed.

"Ye cook yer own supper. And share a bed with two other women. Twopence a night. Any objection?"

"No," said Becky. She was shown into a large shabby room with a fire. A woman was crouched before it, frying a pan of bacon in the flames, and two men were seated at a table, chatting. One of them was looking ruefully at his fingers held in front of him, while the other ate from a dish of stew.

"Ruined they are, shame what pickin' oakum does to fine delicate fingers, innit. No more pickin' pockets after a year inside. You lose the touch."

"You can turn your 'ands to summat else, Joe. Whoa! Who's the newcomer?"

"Miss Swansea." Becky said, taking a seat. She tried to look as if she had been here several times before and knew her way around.

"Welcome, Miss Swansea." said the woman. "I'm Mrs. Glover. What've you got in the bundle, if you don't mind my askin? Anything to sell?"

Becky brightened. She had no money, and she had a few petticoats and an extra shawl; perhaps Mrs. Glover would buy them. She had earrings, and combs and other things that might pay her way.

"So ye're goin' off to Doncaster, then?" said Mrs. Glover later that evening. The room was full now and there was some raucous laughter among a few couples seated in a corner. The fire was still ablaze, and everybody took their turn cooking on it. The room was hot and stuffy. Becky had exchanged a little bread for some tea, and had already sold a green glass necklace for a shilling.

Becky had already received interesting information. Her mother had gone most probably to Doncaster for the St. Leger Races, for Montague went there every year.

"But she's most likely left Doncaster again, if it got too 'ot there for 'im." said Miss Farley, or Janey, as everybody called her.

"Hot?"

"As well as being a gambler, Dickie Montague picks pockets."

Janey was downing gin, and Mrs. Glover showed her a silver cigar case she'd 'come by.' Becky resolved to be very careful of her belongings.

She fell asleep that night in spite of being almost halfway off the mattress, and did not hear the coughs and snores from others. The dormitory was choc-a-bloc. She awoke the following morning and in that fleeting moment between waking and sleeping, did not know where she was. She thought of Daphne straight away – Daphne who was already, on this Monday morning, slaving at the mill, enduring the shouts and sometimes the blows, of the overseer. Becky resolved she'd never work again in a factory or a mill, never submit herself to another person's demands on her time or her freedom. She was free, and was going to find her Ma.

CHAPTER TWENTY-EIGHT

Becky had the fare to Doncaster, but the talk from the lodgers had made her very wary. Montague was a bad character, they said. He had women, commiting crimes and leaving them when the police got hot on his trail. They did not like that she was going after him, she was so young. It was very likely that Montague had involved her mother in cons or thieving. The coppers were always on the lookout for Montague.

Had her mother committed crimes? Becky was very bothered by this. Not only would it be wrong and bad, but what if Mr. Byrd, or Daphne, or Aunt Sarah took it into their heads to come after Becky? What if they asked the police to find her? What if the police, looking for her, found her with her Ma? Mamma could go to jail.

But Becky had no intention of giving up the search for her mother.

"I just have to ensure nobody comes after me, Bounder," she said to the lodging house cat, feeding him a piece of pig's trotter. She thought about writing to Daffy. But Daffy knew her too well and might want more information than she wanted to give. She began to stroke Bounder's head in thought.

"I have it Bounder, at last. Here." she fed him the last of it. He was a fat cat, a good mouser who lived on everybody's scraps as well. He was the only well-nourished being in the house, besides Pug Grainger.

She decided to pay a call to her Aunt's house in Blossom Meadow; that way, the word would get around that looking for her would be a waste of time. She'd tell her she was going to America.

CHAPTER TWENTY-NINE

B ecky became very disheartened in Doncaster. Her
mother was not known anywhere she looked, and
nobody knew the name Richard Montague either.
One woman had laughed at her and told her that some
people had a different name in every city.

Living on the streets had been very exciting for a while, but
not knowing where the next meal was to come from had
long begun to plague her. She was hungry most of the time.
She'd relished the train journey from Manchester, which had
made her feel very grown up, but after a few weeks, the
novelty of freedom had paled. She was getting weak and sad.
All the bravery she'd experienced in Manchester had ebbed
away. She was now living hand to mouth. She fetched and
carried for the other lodgers and hawkers for just a few
pennies every day.

This was a strange city and she did not like it. The people
spoke in a different accent. She did not like being away from
Manchester; she was homesick for the familiar streets, the
shops and even the factory horns, all of which she could
distinguish as belonging to Rowlands, Webster, and the many

others. She feared that the Yorkshire people did not like her and she was insulted because somebody told her that Manchester was a dangerous place.

She was tired of fending off attention from men. Not just young men, but men of all ages. They were ready to pounce on her, a girl alone, and obviously without protection. They offered her drink - gin or beer - which she did not want, memories of her mother's decline disturbing her. She tried to avoid men. They were no good, and she was not about to give any of them the right to rob her of her virtue. She didn't want to end up like old Josephine, worn out, in rags, and reeking of a nasty disease. She'd thought Josephine was about eighty years old but it turned out she was only forty, about the same age as her own mother. Josephine hawked old clothes around the lodging houses, rags that nobody else wanted to sell. She picked them up from rubbish heaps, gave them a desultory wash, and pushed them around in a barrow. Poor Josephine!

She wondered how Daffy was. She supposed she was still living with Mr. Byrd. How could she? He was horrid about their mother and said nasty things. She longed to see Daffy and talk to her. She wanted to write to her – her conscience prickled her. But she was supposed to be in America. Oh how confusing she had made everything! Daffy would want to make her come home, in under Mr. Byrd's roof again, and she was so hungry, she might give in and do that. Then she'd be back in the mill.

She got up and began to walk down the street. It was a fine day, Easter was approaching. The daffodils were out in the gardens she passed. She supposed they were out also in Manchester. Her steps continued. She would go to the railway station and beg there.

"Please Ma'am, 'ave pity!" she said to a lady who gave her only a contemptuous look. Her pleas continued with the passengers disembarking from the London train.

"What are you doin' 'ere? Get out!" Two girls dressed in rags but older than she suddenly appeared from nowhere. "Railway's ours!" They pushed her away. She left in tears, and feeling weak, sat on the pavement, her head in her hands.

"My dear child." She looked up at the gentle voice. A man was patting her shoulder. "I heard that. You mustn't be discouraged. Do you see that building?" he pointed to a tall dark building only a little way off. "Go there. It's the Poor Law Union Workhouse. Knock on the porter's door. Say that Doctor Galsworthy sent you. Do you understand? "

"Yes." she murmured. She did as he instructed. The porter let her in, she was sent to the Receiving room, where she was met by the matron. While not exactly kind, she was efficient in ensuring she was looked after. A woman ran a warm bath for her – the water felt heavenly. They shook white powder into her hair, and took her clothes away. They gave her the workhouse uniform – striped blue dress, black stockings and boots. Then, she was taken to a large dining room where there were hundreds of women filing in to eat. Grace was said, and she devoured the food put in front of her – bread, cheese and milk. That night, she slept in a bed which she had all to herself.

CHAPTER THIRTY

ecky was so happy to have regular meals, clean clothes and a bed that contrary to what she had avowed before, she submitted to all the rules. She was in the Women's Section, and put to work in the laundry. It was very hard work, and some of the soiled linen from the Infirmary made her feel sick. But she didn't balk. The other workers were much older than she; some were mothers and their children were in another Section. Some were simple-minded. But there was nobody her own age at all.

After she had been there several weeks, she was summoned to Matron's office.

"Becky, the Board of Guardians have decided to apprentice you out," she said. "All of the young women go into service. We've found you a place near Edenthorpe, a small farmhouse with only one other house servant. You will be furnished with new clothes and boots and every necessity."

Becky was stricken.

"I wanted to stay here a while longer." she said.

"Goodness no. An able-bodied young woman like yourself has to learn to make her way in the world. This is a good start for you. We'll arrange the transport and give you enough money to see you on your way – your way to your new life, Miss Swansea."

CHAPTER THIRTY-ONE

Mrs. Webster was almost too weak to raise her head, let alone speak. The dreaded disease had slowly taken over her body and sapped her strength.

It was Ethan's turn to keep vigil by her bedside, and he held her hand. The gaslight gave out eerie shadows. The nurse slept in a chair, he would awaken her if there was any change. His father had been persuaded to take some rest. The girls were exhausted and spent with grief, they had retired to their apartments for a few hours.

"Ethan," she said, opening her eyes.

He bent towards her.

"Mamma! What is it? What do you need?"

"Please do as your father asks. He wants your good. You must marry. A sensible girl, with a good heart, will be the making of you. Promise?"

He could not refuse this request, though he felt very put-out. Marriage was the last thing he wanted!

"Very well, Mamma. I will do my best."

"I know you will. Your father wants your good."

"Yes, Mamma." Ethan did not know why she spoke thus of his father, who was still making exorbitant demands on his time and energy. He still hated the Mill, hated going there, and skipped off as often as he could on some pretext or other.

CHAPTER THIRTY-TWO

"**P**oor Mrs. Webster is gone." said Mr. Byrd later that day, upon receiving a message. He and Daphne went to the house to sympathise. She always felt a little shy of the Websters and said little, but her sincere demeanour and her kind eyes said as much as needed to be said. The Misses Webster thanked her graciously for her sympathy and tea was served to them in the drawing room. Thank Goodness none of them asked for her mother! They must know, however, all that had happened. They did ask for Miss Becky, to which she replied that she was unable to attend them that day.

Mr. Ethan also thanked her kindly for coming. He was even more handsome than she had remembered. He was very cordial to her.

They went to the funeral the following day, and afterwards joined them in a repast at their home. Again, the sisters were friendly and seemed to appreciate her support, and she felt herself drawn to their brother, in spite of herself. She knew he was wild and was always getting into scrapes. But was there not good in him too? His dark hair fell over his forehead and his green eyes were soulful. He seemed lost. She couldn't make up her mind as to the exact colour of his eyes. They were a dark green, she thought. Almost brown but not quite.

She thought that her watching him had gone unnoticed, and would have been humiliated to find that Mr. Webster had seen her interest, and astonished if she had known his thoughts.

CHAPTER THIRTY-THREE

"Mr. Webster and the young Master are coming to Sunday dinner," Mr. Byrd announced one day in the middle of the week. "I want your best cooking. I have a liking for your roast beef, and potatoes done around the joint. And for dessert, what about that pudding you cooked last week?"

"It sounds like a feast," said Daphne astonished. Ethan was coming too! Her heart fluttered a little. She was a whirl of preparation on Saturday evening making the pudding, and Sunday morning, up early to put the joint over the fire. Mr. Byrd had chosen it at the butchers. She took an hour off to go to church; she didn't feel right for the day if she didn't keep Sunday holy. She'd made friends there too, and walked back with them.

Mr. Webster arrived on Sunday at noon, his sulky son in tow. It was obvious that this was an imposition on Ethan. The table was laid very nicely, and Mr. Byrd carved. She was nervous as the guests tucked in. The roast beef and potatoes were excellently done, the gravy full of flavour and the brussel sprouts tender. Mr. Webster ate heartily, Ethan seemed almost reluctant to tackle his plate, but did eat up as much as his father did, and took some more beef when offered.

"That was excellent fare, Miss Swansea," Mr. Webster said, after making short work of the pudding smothered in custard. "I must compliment you. What about it, Ethan, eh?"

Ethan only grunted his agreement, which Daphne thought rude. She was hurt at his sullenness and his lack of effort at conversation. Perhaps he was thinking of his mother and how much he missed her. She wished she could justify his manners.

Daphne washed the dishes, pots and pans and as soon as they were all back in their proper places, she sat down to rest for a while before taking a walk.

Mr. Byrd was reading the paper, but he put it down.

"I want to talk to you, Daphne."

Daphne sighed. Whatever it was, it was probably not something she wished to hear. But nothing could have prepared her for what her stepfather had to say.

"You'll be seventeen next May, and Mr. Webster and I have decided that you will marry Master Webster."

Daphne was floored. Just like that, he tells her that her future is decided! A multitude of emotions flew through her. Shock, anger, resentment and even the hope of love mingled together in a strange tempest whirling about her head.

"There's bad times ahead at the mill, on account the American Civil War. The South is at war with the North, and the fields are abandoned and there will be far less cotton coming over, and many hands will be turned off. So, Daphne, you've to marry. And Mr. Webster wants Ethan to have a wife, and he took a liking to you. It all fell into place very conveniently. We agreed on you marrying next May then. I'll keep you till then, never fear, for you are to work no more; Mr. Webster won't have his future daughter-in-law working."

"Father, that – that is – what does Master Webster think? Does he even know? I don't know if he even likes me!"

Daphne thought privately that Ethan did not like her at all, and her heart sank.

"Why, that's of no matter. I liked your mother, and what happened? You might as well dislike your spouse on your wedding day as like." He rattled the paper.

"I'm flummoxed." was all Daphne could say. "I'm to marry! I don't know what to say, what to feel about it. And – you fixed it without telling me! Asking me!"

"You might thank me," said her stepfather. "There's not many would take you, with your mother a bolter, and nothing to your name. I've done what I can for you, and I hope you'll have me to Sunday dinner. I don't know what I'll do the other days, get a housekeeper cheap, I suppose. I'm never marrying again, that's for sure, even if I was free of your mother."

Daphne was dumbfounded. Words eluded her. Her stepfather sat up suddenly, the paper again in front of his face.

"Ha! Listen here! It seems we'll get cotton, from Bengal, but as yet, nothing is set up. They're looking into it. And it'd only be a mite compared to America, not enough to keep the engines going, to my mind."

Daphne pulled her cloak around her and left Mr. Byrd, his newspaper, his cotton and his engines. It did not occur to her to refuse his scheme. Ethan was to be her husband – he would of course fall in love with her, would he not? She knew she was halfway in love with him, and now, it seemed she'd been catapulted in all the way, for now she might as well give him her entire heart! And it would be unthinkable that he would not love her *now*. He must not know yet, or he would have paid her some kind attentions today.

She wished she knew where Becky was! She wanted so much to tell her sister about this turn her life was to take! She burned to talk to somebody, and decided to walk to Blossom Meadow to see Aunt Sarah.

CHAPTER THIRTY-FOUR

It had been two years at least since she'd been in Blossom Meadow. Her mother had never wanted to go back there. She and her sister had written for a while, but Sarah was a very poor correspondent, and there hadn't been much news.

She visited Gabriel's grave first, or at least the one she thought was his. There was no headstone, not even a marker. Soon after she was knocking on her aunt's door in the narrow, damp street.

Her cousin June opened it, and was delighted to see her.

Uncle Ted was sitting by the fire, smoking a pipe. He did not get up, but waved his hand in greeting. The room was smoky and dark.

Daphne looked about. "Is Aunt Sarah out?"

"Why, no, Daffy, you didna hear the bad news. We didna know where you were, you moved so much. Ma's gone these three months past. Her and Louisa. Cholera. Here, sit down. It's a shock, I know. She was well on Tuesday, and gone

Wednesday night, Louisa was nursing her more than me, she caught it too, and was gone by Saturday."

"Put on some tea, June, will you." said her uncle. "Your cousin need a cuppa."

For the second time that day Daphne was lost for words, this time in grief. What a curse this place was! Tears rolled down her cheeks as she held her head in her hands.

She sipped her tea from the only matching cup and saucer in the flat, reserved for a visitor.

"Any word of your Ma?" asked June.

"You know she did a bolt, then?"

"Becky told us."

"Becky! Did you see her?"

June looked a little awkward, and Daphne saw her avert her eyes.

"I'll go out awhile," her uncle said, throwing back the rest of his tea and taking his cap and coat from the doornail. The door slammed behind him.

"What's the matter?" Daphne had a sick feeling.

"Becky was 'ere one day. She din't write to tell you, then? She said she was off to America, with a family she was workin' for. Off to New York."

"Off to America," said Daphne, fresh tears filling her eyes. "America! She's as good as dead, if she's all that way gone. I'll never see her again." She put her arms on the table and laid her head on them, sobbing her heart out.

"When was that?"

"Oh – maybe a year ago." June was very vague. "Did she not write an' tell you hersel'?

Daphne shook her head.

"I can't understand why she didn't do that," she said.

"And I've a mind to go, myself," said her cousin, after a long pause. "Tha's why Pa left the 'ouse just now. 'E's dead against it. But what's 'ere? Nothing! You know, I 'eard you get a lot to eat on the ship. Three meals a day. And no work at all to do during the voyage, only lark about the decks, an' dancin' i' th'evenings. Some meets their true loves on board. Oh, don't take on so bad, Daffy! Have you any good news for me? There must be some about!"

Daphne told her of her impending marriage, but kept her true feelings, her doubts to herself. June was overjoyed at her doing so well, and congratulated her over and over on making such a great conquest, that she hadn't the heart to tell her how it was all arranged, and how she feared that her fiancé did not like her.

"You've brightened my week," June said. "Wait till I tell everyone! You lucky, lucky girl! I'm so glad someone 'as some luck! Maybe I won't go to America after all. Could you find me a job, in your 'ouse? I'll do anything!"

CHAPTER THIRTY-FIVE

Winter was hard for many people with no work, or with reduced hours. Daphne kept herself busy at home, sewing her trousseau. Her stepfather advanced her money for materials, and she had to be very economical as to how she used what she had, cutting out very carefully to leave enough leftover fabric for making embellishments such as flounces.

During the time of their engagement, she and her fiancé met at Christmas. She found him cold and her heart sank. His sisters, who had been very cordial to her in recent times, had reverted to their superior airs and beyond what was demanded by politeness, ignored her.

"I don't understand how he has consented to marry me." she said in despair to Mr. Byrd.

"His father wishes it, that's how. And his mother. He won't go against the wishes of his dying mother."

"He doesn't like me, Father. I feel it's a mistake!"

"There's no mistake, Daffy. Like or not, you two are to be married."

They met again a few times before the wedding, and Daphne was not reassured. He did not begin conversations; she did. He gave monosyllabic answers, and she soon gave up. Perhaps after the wedding, after they had spent days and nights in each other's company, his love would be awakened.

She sewed her wedding dress with her friends from church helping her. Her heart ached for her mother and Becky. Why had Becky run off to America without telling her? She could not understand it! As for her mother, she wished she knew where she was – what daughter could get married without her own mother knowing about it?

On a mild May morning just after her birthday, Daphne became Mrs. Webster. The couple posed for the photographer outside the church, and the Wedding Breakfast followed in her new home. Kitty helped Daphne change into her travelling costume, and the newlyweds were waved off to Blackpool. She and her husband were alone at last. She looked across at him in the train carriage. He was not looking at her; he was looking everywhere but at her. Her heart sank deep in her chest. This was an absolutely horrid state of things! He wasn't even trying to like her! She gave up attempts at conversation and stared out the window. Anybody watching them, she thought, would have decided that they were going to a funeral.

Her wedding night brought no joy. He showed no affection or tenderness, just indifference, and after he had done his duty left her to get dressed and he went out into the

Blackpool night, presumably to sample what it had to offer. Daphne buried her head in her pillow and cried, heartbroken, stifling her sobs so that the people in the next room would not hear.

She felt she was the loneliest bride in the world.

CHAPTER THIRTY-SIX

The following morning was Sunday; he had not returned. Looking out the window she saw the sea, grey and still in the gathering light. Last evening, she had seen a church very near. Why should she wait for him to come back, before she went out? God was calling her to come to Him to be consoled with the words and the bread of life. God would never reject her as her husband did, that she knew.

She soaked up the readings. *I will never forget you...I have carved you upon the palms of my hands...*what a tremendous promise from our Father-God!

The next days were very difficult. Daphne saw her husband for only a few minutes every day. She took her meals alone; she walked alone on the pier; she slept alone after he had fulfilled his marital duty.

"Are you not pleased with me?" she asked him one night as he left to go out.

"I want you to understand one thing," he said. "I was forced into this. I will do my duty. Expect no more."

"Do you think I had a choice too?" she flared a little. He seemed surprised.

"But you have done very well for yourself." he pointed out.

"Have I? Without affection, it's nothing to me." she said in a lower tone. "Are you – are you in love with somebody else, Ethan?"

"No."

She believed him.

"Why then, can you not even try to make this marriage one of love rather than coldness?"

"No"

"Why?"

"Because this marriage was against my will. But my father threatened to cut me off if I did not go for it."

He sat on the bed beside her and stared at her.

"You are a comely young woman, Daphne. Your hair and eyes are uncommonly good. In different circumstances, I could perhaps - but the way things are, can you expect me to be happy at your inferior state in life? Your connections are so very low! *Who is your mother? What is your mother?*"

"Whoever, and whatever my mother is, my father is a hero. He gave his life so someone else could live."

"Your father might have become somebody had he lived, I will grant him that."

"Why do you leave me here alone every night?" she asked him. "Please don't go out. Stay, and we can talk."

"I fear we have nothing to talk of." he said, putting on his coat. "I do not mean you to get grieved about this, by the way.

I do not mean to make you unhappy, Daphne. I'm not a devil. I will go my way, and you may go yours. Do you know what I mean? Once we have an heir, of course."

"That's the most horrible thing I ever heard of!"

He gave a long-suffering sigh.

"I have important friends. Peers, some of them. I hoped to marry the sister of one. Any of them. My father did not understand. I have a wife now who has a flat tone in her accent, and has called one of England's worst slums home. What if they find out? I'd be a laughing-stock. How can I accept invitations to dinner parties and balls, when you don't even know how to dance a quadrille, I'll bet."

"I can learn to speak better, and I can learn to dance!" she said tearfully, the pain inside growing.

"It's of no account. They will all know the moment they see you that you're not of our rank. I cannot see them anymore; I have cut them all off, before they cut me. My marriage to you has ruined my life."

He put on his hat and left.

His cruelty seared her and that night, she felt herself in grave danger of falling into hatred of him. No, surely not!

There was only one thing to do, and that was to pray for him with every thought she had of him. Otherwise, an ugly poison would enter her mind and begin to rot her soul. She could not allow that to happen. Never!

Lord, I place myself into Your hands. Do with me as You will.

CHAPTER THIRTY-SEVEN

"**T**hey are come," said Lavinia, looking out the window at the carriage turning in the gate. "And, I hate to say so, but Papa is going out to meet them."

"Papa has lost his mind." said her sister Helena, putting down her book. "But Livvy, he said we are to help her."

"I'm not helping her! Neither are you! She's intruding here. Let her find her own way through the mysteries of housekeeping and dealing with the servants, and perhaps she will go back to where she belongs. She takes precedence over us, you know."

"That's insufferable. Look, Ethan is helping her from the carriage. He hasn't fallen in love with her, has he?" Helena had a smidgen of a romantic spirit, and occasionally felt a little chink in her resolve to reject her new sister-in-law, but Lavinia was quick to spot it and crush it before it came to anything.

"No, how could he? He has to play the part, opposite Papa and the servants. Now, let us both curtsey very deeply when she comes in, it will both confuse and humble her."

The two girls were standing to greet the new Mrs. Webster, and they curtsied as if greeting Royalty. They saw Daphne flush and look bewildered, and were pleased. They greeted their brother with a kiss. He then took his leave and went upstairs.

For the remainder of the evening, Daphne felt she was an outcast. The following morning, she was humiliated again. She had come down alone to breakfast because Ethan had left the house early. The sisters were seated, eating ham and eggs and toast, and she seated herself also, and waited for a servant to appear. She had always been served at table in this house; it was the way it was done. She saw a smirk pass from one sister to another, and didn't know why. Then she noticed the covered platters on the sideboard. Mr. Webster came in at that moment, said a hearty 'Good morning!' went straight to the platters and helped himself. As she got up to awkwardly follow him, she heard Lavinia snigger.

In the morning room, a basket of mending was waiting, and Lavinia took up one of her father's shirts. Daphne took one she thought might be Ethan's. Helena was reading a book by the window. Thrown upon the table was a bunch of keys and a pouch. She did not take any notice of them.

"Do you like to read, Daphne?" asked Lavinia in a condescending fashion.

"No, not much."

"Oh come, I'm sure you are a great reader. Helena, give Daphne your book, and she will read to us."

"But I – " began Helena, but then seeing Lavinia's intention, handed the book to Daphne. It was '*Pamela*' by Samuel Richardson. Reluctantly, Daphne took it up, read a few lines rather awkwardly, as if before a stern schoolteacher. Then she stopped abruptly.

"This is indecent." she said, closing it and setting it on the table, blushing.

"Helena. How could you?" asked Lavinia, in mock censure.

"Oh, you've lost my place," Helena complained, taking up the book again.

Daphne returned to her mending.

After a few minutes, there was a knock on the door, and Cook appeared, looking very apologetic. She addressed herself to Lavinia.

"I'm sorry Miss Webster, but I a'nt got any Orders for today. If I don't get them soon, the butchers will not have anything worth eating."

"Well, Cook, that is not my concern anymore." said Lavinia coolly.

Mrs. Carroll looked directly at Daphne.

A deep blush crept over the new Mrs. Webster's cheeks. Mrs. Carroll saw her discomfort and looked down.

"Do you want help?" asked Lavinia of Daphne in a very superior tone, as if she were the most tiresome creature in the world.

"Yes, please, I'm sorry, I didn't know. "

Lavinia cast her eyes to the ceiling and put down her sewing.

"Every morning after breakfast, you are to go down to the kitchen and give Cook her orders." Lavinia said slowly, as if Daphne were a person of limited intelligence. "And if you're wondering what that bunch of keys is for, it's yours now. You are to run the house, hold the keys to the stores, and give Cook what she requires. Beside the keys you will see a pouch containing money. I have held that since Mamma died. Now, it's yours to manage. I hope you can manage money *wisely*?"

Helena sniggered. Daphne knew that the remark was meant to be a dig at her mother.

"I see, I am so sorry –" Daphne got up, took the keys and pouch and left the room with Cook. Her hands were trembling with emotion. Following Cook downstairs, she felt that she had entered a nightmare. Her sisters-in-law were horrible people! Why had they not instructed her as to her duties?

Cook was very kind and helpful to her, and told her they always had liver and onions on Thursdays, with apple crumble to follow. Daphne took the opportunity of telling her to do whatever she was used to doing on the different days of the week, nothing should change. She was trembling all over with distress. Afterward, she did not go back to the morning room, but went outside and walked in the back garden, found a copse of trees with a pavilion secluded among them, went in, sat down and cried bitterly.

If she could have heard Cook speak to the housemaid Kitty after she had left the kitchen, she would have been gratified to know that in her opinion Miss Lavinia Webster was the nastiest woman ever born and Miss Helena was led and said by her, and poor young Mrs. Webster was going to suffer hell on earth until the two of them found husbands, which, in Cooks opinion, would never be, for what man in his wits would saddle himself with either of them?

CHAPTER THIRTY-EIGHT

Becky was a maid-of-all-work on a farm deep in the moors in a ramshackle farmhouse that seemed to shake to its foundations with every wind that blew. Her mistress was Mrs. Parker, and very fussy. She felt very isolated; there was nobody else her own age; the cook was an old woman. She was very wary around the farmhands and stablemen as the penalty for having followers was instant dismissal without a character reference. Leo, one of the dairymen, was friendly but Mrs. Parker lectured her for idleness when she was caught talking to him, and after that she was looked upon with great suspicion and was timed whenever her chores took her outside. Summer was not too bad, autumn, when it came, brought the wind, but winter, when it came, was cruel. The silent moors were menacing and desolate. Becky found no joy in the sparkles the sun made on the frost, she knew only that her fingers were numb and frozen. Sometimes it rained for days on end and the wind screamed and howled around her little room under the roof, rattling the window hard. She did not believe in fairies, but on eerie nights when she was drifting off to sleep, she sometimes half-dreamed that goblins were trying to smash their way in, and woke up again, frightened.

Every morning she heard a train whistle in the distance and wished she could run and get on one that would take her to a town. She was a city girl.

She began to think almost with longing of the streets again, the easy laughter and company there, the jokes and camaraderie, even if you had to sleep three to a bed and watch your back all the time. But she had good food to eat, as much as she wanted, and she did not ever want to be hungry again, so she put up with it for now. There were no shops or fairs nearby to spend her money on, and she was surprised that she was able to save it. When she had a little more saved, she thought, she'd go home again.

At last, she decided that Daphne should know she was still in England. How daft she had been, to think that she could fool everybody!

CHAPTER THIRTY-NINE

M r. Byrd scrutinised the letter when it came. This girlish hand could only be from Becky Swansea. He had no scruple in opening it. The Swanseas would always be in debt to him and he felt that justified him in knowing all their business.

Dear Daffy,

I hope you are well. You will be surprised this letter was posted in England. Did you hear I was off to America?? Forgive me but I only said that to stop the Whisker sending someone to find me. I went to Doncaster and looked for Mamma but did not find her. I lived on the streets and then was taken in by the workhouse, and then they sent me here, to this farm, I hate it here, it's the middle of nowhere, and I want to <u>come home soon</u>. Do you still work at the Mill. Please write back soon. I have to go, she wants her tea now,

Love Becky xxxxx

Mr. Byrd was very glad he opened the letter though to read of himself referred to as 'The Whisker' put him out of sorts. After all he had done for those wenches! She had been on the streets and lived in the workhouse – he could not allow

Daphne to renew such a connection as that, when she was getting on so well with the Websters. He crushed the letter and threw it into the fire.

He did the same thing with two more letters that arrived from Becky, and then the letters stopped.

CHAPTER FORTY

"There's someone at back door to see you, Ma'am." said Kitty one afternoon. "Shall I send her up?"

Lavinia and Helena had gone for a walk, and Daphne was alone in the drawing room.

A few minutes later, the door opened and Kitty announced 'Miss Bridges'. It was her cousin June!

She rushed forward to hug her, but June's eyes were on her surroundings more than on her.

"Why, cousin, you 'ave done very well for yourself!" she stood awkwardly on the hearthrug.

"Sit down," urged Daphne, indicating a chair. June sat, reluctantly, on one of the velvet-covered chairs. She shook her head in wonder.

"This is oceans away from where we live, isn't it?" she said wonderingly. She was poised awkwardly on the edge of the chair.

"Be easy, June. I'm still your cousin Daffy."

"I know, an' you 'aven't changed, happy to say. I am flummoxed at this posh place. It's like a palace."

"Would you like some tea?" Daphne got up.

"Oh no, no! I'd be terrified!"

"Fiddlesticks!" Daphne rang the bell.

"Are you still thinking about America?"

"I don't think so. Not with the war over there an' all. I'll chance my luck 'ere." June waited expectantly.

"Would you like to work here then? In this house?"

"There's nothing I'd like better, I'm sure!"

"What about a housemaid? Light the fires, dust, sweep?"

"I can do all that."

"It's yours, then."

"Is that your weddin' photo?" June picked up the silver-framed photograph that graced a little table. "Ooh, he is 'andsome, I say. Your 'andsome prince!"

Daphne merely smiled.

June had just finished her second cup of tea when Daphne espied through the window, her sisters-in-law come in the gate.

"Are they –?" asked June, following her gaze.

"Yes."

"Are they nice to you?"

"No, not at all."

"When I'm housemaid, I'll let spiders loose in their beds. Oh, tha' was good tea! The best ever! Will I get to drink tha' when I work here? When will I begin then?"

"Anytime you like. I'll see you down the stairs and walk with you to the back gate." She jumped up. She had no wish to see her sisters-in-law, now heading for the front door, and wanted to drag out the visit with her cousin as long as she could.

Mr. Webster was surprised that she had engaged another housemaid…it seemed to him a waste of money…the house was very well staffed…oh, she needed a job, did she? And she was a cousin? He seemed to think about that for a while, a little displeased. Lavinia and Helena were full of amused contempt, and Ethan looked angry.

"Employing your relations is not the thing to do," he said. "There's no need to advertise your low connections to the servants."

As it happened, Jane's employment did not last long. Six weeks later, she gave notice. The sisters were very nasty to her, she said, and the kitchen staff were afraid she was telling tales upstairs. She was on her way. Would Daffy give her a character? Daffy obliged, and wrote her an excellent reference.

CHAPTER FORTY-ONE

I t was the most miserable summer in Daphne's life, and the realisation a few months after her marriage that she was with child, did not make her happy. She wished to be sure before she told Ethan. But soon there was no disguising it, and she told him. He was very pleased.

"An heir on the way, by Jove, that's capital! Good for you, Daphne! An heir!"

Daphne remembered what he had said in Blackpool, and felt that if the child was a boy, that she would be even less loved and more neglected than now, if that were possible. She sank into a state of sadness.

"We can't allow her to be dejected like this," said Lavinia unexpectedly one day to her sister as they walked in the garden. They could see Daphne in the pavilion, and she was sitting with her head down, and her hands folded on her lap, the picture of sadness.

"What, Livvy? You don't want her to be happy, do you? You said –"

"Oh, it isn't for her sake, Helena. It's for the child's. If she's unhappy, the child will be a great trouble to us. You know why an expectant mother should never visit a zoological gardens, do you not? If she takes fright at an animal, the child may have some of the characteristics of that animal, like ears that stick out like an elephant's."

Helena was not inclined to believe this.

"So if she is sad, the child will have a melancholy nature. So we have to be nice to her until her lying-in. Of course, she might not survive childbirth." she whispered, with a little glee.

"Many women die." said Helena.

Both sisters realised what they were thinking, but only Helena felt guilty at her thoughts.

Daphne however was pleasantly surprised to find her needs and comforts attended to by her two sisters-in-law. Perhaps they simply needed time to get to know her! She was still praying a great deal, not even formal prayers, but was trying to develop a trusting heart, and whenever she felt sad or in doubt or her cross felt heavier than usual, she raised her eyes in trust. It did not always alleviate her pain, but she knew it was the right thing to do. Along with trust, she was trying to be grateful for what she had. Food, regular, nourishing food. Warm fires. Strong boots and good clothes – more than she could wear, as Ethan had instructed her to go and have some good clothes made. He was generous with money. A dancing master had been employed as a woman in her position needed to know the fashionable dances, and an elocution master tempered her strong Mancunian accent. By Christmas she was ready for the various invitations and amusements the season would bring, but England was in a sober mood, and in mourning, for Prince Albert had died of typhoid fever just beforehand.

CHAPTER FORTY-TWO

arly in March, Daphne felt pains. She said nothing for a time – again wanting to be sure – but there was no mistaking that her body had embarked on a mission of its own, over which she had no control, and the contractions came with regularity. She retired to the upstairs bedroom, and the doctor was sent for.

Lavinia and Helena sat downstairs all that evening, waiting for the labour to be over, getting more impatient at every hour that passed. Ethan paced the hall, their father told them all to be patient. He had been through this several times, with the three he had, and two lost.

Upstairs, Daphne felt that she was in the grip of something powerful, relentless and agonising. The pain was unbearable! She couldn't take any more of it, was utterly helpless in its teeth and as the night wore on, she began to wonder if death would be preferable. Why did the Lord God permit this to be so hard? The midwife consoled her and urged her to be brave, the doctor examined her every now and then, and told her that 'Nature must take its course', which did nothing to comfort her at all.

The girls retired to bed. Helena was tearful and Lavinia told her not to be a goose, she was sure that Daphne was fussing about nothing, women had babies all the time.

Mr. Webster summoned the doctor downstairs at about 3am, Ethan by his side.

"How is she?"

"It's a hard labour. Not uncommon for a first time mother. But in her case, harder than I like to see. Very slow progress."

"Can you give her anything? Chloroform?"

"I am not in favour of chloroform." He said stiffly. He wished that the Queen had never used it. Now mothers were asking for it all the time, and he believed its safety had not been properly evaluated. "Besides, it would not hurry things along."

"Is there any danger to the child?" Ethan asked.

"Why of course, the longer it goes on, the more the child is at risk."

"I insist you hurry up her labour!" snapped Ethan.

"There is nothing I can do to hurry up her labour, sir. Nature must take its course. It might help her," he addressed Ethan. "If you were to give her a word of encouragement. I will allow you into the room. Tell her that everything will be all right. Sometimes, all a young mother needs is a word from her husband that everything is in hand. I do not usually allow husbands in, but in the poorer areas of the city, it is more difficult to keep them out, and I've often noticed that after a husband has barged in and spoken words of love and tenderness to his wife, however inebriated he may be, that she calms herself and gets on much better. Come along, Mr. Ethan."

Ethan was terrified at the thought of going into the room, but his father rapped that he was to do what the doctor said, and practically pushed him in the room.

Daphne was lying on the bed under a sheet and looked ghastly; pale, glowing with perspiration, her hair in damp strands about her face. Her expression showed her distress. The midwife was by her side.

"Daphne, old girl." he began, at her bedside.

"Ethan!" she looked at him, with surprised gratitude, and her eyes filled with tears. He felt very awkward.

"Look here, you're doing fine."

"No, I'm not. It's been all day and all night. I'm exhausted – so tired now."

Ethan did not know what to say next.

"Don't give up, Mrs. Webster," said the doctor, for him.

"Yes, he's right, you know! Don't give up! You're plucky! Hang on, Daffy."

"Daffy." She repeated her name and smiled wanly. He took her hand and stroked it.

"Do you think so, Ethan? It's so hard. I'm so tired, Ethan. I want to go to sleep." she closed her eyes, pressing his hand against her cheek.

He pinched her cheek. "It won't take long, if you pluck up your courage. This time tomorrow, we'll have a son. Only you'll have to keep at it."

"Keep at it?" Suddenly she was seized with a pain and cried out in great distress. Ethan paled. She would die. She would. And she'd never had any love from him. He saw her dead in her coffin, and his bitter regret then, that he'd never even tried to love her! She was a beautiful girl with a beautiful nature, a soft heart and all she wanted from him was to be loved! He had denied her that. He threw his arms about her.

"Daffy! Don't die. You hear me? Just don't. I want you. I love you."

He held her until the contraction subsided.

"What did you say?"

"I – I said I love you," he stammered. "You will do it, won't you? You'll get through this – get better?"

"I will try." she said.

"You must leave now." said the doctor as he approached.

Ethan kissed her, softly tucked a few strands of hair behind her ear, and left.

"I hope she's going to be all right," he said to his father, who was lingering on the landing. He went downstairs at a rapid pace. All this did not seem real. A woman, fighting for her life bringing a child into the world.

He went to his room and prayed fervently. *'Lord, I have been a bad fellow, a bounder, a disobedient son, and a selfish and cruel husband. I will change, only spare Daphne!'*

Daphne delivered her child at six o'clock that morning. A dreadful silence enveloped the bedchamber. No baby's cry broke through to delight the attendants and those waiting downstairs. Her little son was stillborn.

CHAPTER FORTY-THREE

The shock of what had happened affected the entire household in different ways. Ethan became angry and bitter, until Mr. Webster reminded him that his older brother had died a mere five minutes after birth. "Your mother and I got over it," he said. "You will too. You have to."

Lavinia was filled with silent contempt. Her stupid sister-in-law could not even bring a child safely into the world! Her nephew – a darling little fellow the image of Ethan - was dead and it was her fault. Helena wanted to be nice to Daphne but she feared Lavinia so much that she did not dare.

Daphne fell into a deep sleep after her long, hard labour and the sorrow at the end of it. There was meant to be joy, but there was grief. Only grief, and the memory of those long, long hours of pain – all in vain. She woke up towards evening, and remembered immediately what had happened, with a dart of pain in her heart. But Ethan was there.

"I'm sorry." she said, as soon as she opened her eyes.

CHAPTER FORTY-FOUR

Ethan was more disappointed than he pretended. Though understanding that Daphne had done the best she could to bring forth the child, and that she was not to be blamed in any way for this catastrophe, he had a weak mind, and the tenderness he had felt for her might have been nurtured, if he had not been so selfish and pitied himself so much. His resolve was quickly forgotten, God had spared Daphne, yes, but had taken his son! He prayed no more.

Another of Ethan's weaknesses was his desire to hob-nob, and after his great disappointment had faded a little, the idea that Daphne was in his way began to come to the fore again.

Several months later, he bumped into three of his old friends one day at Victoria Station.

"Where have you been, old man?" asked Lord Longstone, slapping his shoulder.

"You got married, and we've never even seen your bride – why are you hiding her away?"

"This won't do, Webster. Won't do. We shall see about it."

A few weeks later an invitation arrived for Mr. and Mrs. Webster to attend a house party, to last one week, at Longstone Park, near the Peak District. This threw Ethan into a great mood – his wife was not holding him back after all – Longstone must know that she was not of any significant family. Daphne was both thrilled at the change of scenery, especially being in the country, and afraid of whether she would be good enough for the rest of the guests. Lavinia was thrown into fits of anger and jealousy, and Helena followed suit. They would not help her to get ready, not in the slightest way. Daphne had to get three evening gowns made, and all the accessories, and several morning and carriage gowns.

"Every woman there will have a lady's maid, you'll be terribly looked down upon," sniffed Lavinia. "And with frequent changes of gowns, who is going to wash for you? You cannot go down to the servant's hall at night to wash out your linens!"

"I will bring enough, then." said Daphne, "Thank you for telling me."

Lavinia was cross that she had been inadvertently helpful to her, and not made her feel inadequate to the situation.

CHAPTER FORTY-FIVE

Ethan was in wonderful form as they neared Longstone Park. He had never been invited there, and was very proud to be included in a house party, of all things! He talked of the grand setting, the woods, the canal, and the family who lived there. He dispensed advice to Daphne all the way there, a list of 'dos' and 'don'ts' that she was quite frightened by the time the fine Georgian mansion came into view around a corner of the driveway.

"Look and act as if you're used to all this, as if you've moved in these circles all your life," he instructed her.

"I will do my best. I won't disgrace you, I promise."

"It would be better not to speak on things you know nothing of. Most of the women you meet will have travelled abroad. Father was too miserly to send me anywhere, but I've read up about Rome and Zurich and all those places. You do know where they are, don't you?"

"Rome is in Italy, and Zurich is in Switzerland."

"That's good! Where is St. Petersburg?"

"It's in Russia! Ethan, I had six years of schooling!"

"I did not know." he looked astonished.

"You never talk to me, that's why you didn't know." She looked out the window.

"I am glad to hear it, but all the same, do not talk of your childhood. Make yourself agreeable of course, but there's no need to prattle on. You'll be found out."

Daphne said a silent prayer.

They were ushered up the steps by a footman, their luggage taken away by two more. Inside, Daphne found an array of people in the lofty Hall waiting to greet them. *The Family!* She was surprised because they did not seem at all as intimidating as she had feared, or as Ethan had led her to believe. They were friendly, though they glided about and spoke posh; Lord Longstone made her feel very welcome, kissing her hand and complimenting her. The Honourable Ellen Longstone, his sister, asked her if she had brought her maid – "er, no" she answered breathlessly. That was no problem! She'd ask Mrs. Beets, the housekeeper, to assign a housemaid to her. Lady Ellen seemed so unlike Lavinia that Daphne was astonished. She had an easy, open nature and smiled a great deal.

She'd make Ethan proud of her this week, she would, she thought as she climbed the stairs to their room, a handsomely-fitted lavender and grey, the loveliest room she had ever laid eyes on. The window looked out on a clear blue lake and beyond miles of rolling green fields, a row of soft purple peaks rose to the sky. A housemaid soon appeared to unpack her clothes and to help her get ready for dinner; a footman performed the same service for Ethan.

"Will we ever be rich like this?" he said, as they made their way downstairs. "You look very pretty, by the way! I do not know who we will be meeting here, Daphne, so be careful and don't let your guard down, eh?"

The drawing room was filled with chattering guests, and Daphne had never seen so much style or jewellery on any set of people. The Longstones must be some of the richest people in England! Ethan found her a seat, and she looked about her. The room was buzzing with conversation, but a voice near her made her suddenly freeze. A woman's voice, unchanged with the years. She dared not look about! The voice was speaking to Lady Longstone, the widowed mother of Lord Longstone. The woman moved a little to her side, in full view, and finally Daphne confirmed what she had suspected – Mrs. Havershall, in a midnight-blue gown and pearls, stood a little way off, speaking animatedly to her hostess.

Had she been recognised as well? Surely not – she was only a girl when Mrs. Havershall had last seen her. She would try to stay out of her way. But her heart beat fast for a little while, until they were all called into dinner.

She was seated with a young man on her left and an older man on her right. Mrs. Havershall was far away from her, close to the head of the table, beside Lady Longstone. Ethan was across from her. He made eyes at her to speak to the man on her right and she realised that she was supposed to initiate the conversation. Oh, such silly - hard rules! She did not know what to say, so she turned to him and spoke of the weather. How safe weather was! You could not let yourself down talking of rain and sun!

Mr. Reed was quite talkative, but after the main course Ethan signalled to her to speak to the man on the other side. Again, the weather came to her rescue.

The women withdrew, and Daphne did her best to avoid Mrs. Havershall, but to her dismay found that the lady's eyes flicked toward her more than once.

"Oh, that is Mrs. Webster," said Lady Longstone, seeing the direction of her look. "The wife of Mr. Ethan Webster."

Daphne nodded her greeting, her eyes down.

"Have we met before?" asked Mrs. Havershall. "You put me in mind of someone. I cannot think who!"

Daphne shook her head.

"I don't think so," she murmured, in a soft voice.

"Perhaps I have not met you, but perhaps I am acquainted with your mother," persisted the older woman, peering at her. "Pray tell me, what is your maiden name?"

"You must excuse me for stealing Mrs. Webster away directly," interrupted Lady Ellen, touching Daphne's elbow. "But I must ask her to turn the pages for me while I play." She led the way to the piano and Daphne got up directly to follow her, nodding to Mrs. Havershall, whose gaze followed. Thank goodness she'd learned how to read music at school; she had turned pages for Becky. She was occupied with Ellen until the men joined them, and Ethan looked very satisfied to see that she had made herself useful to Lord Longstone's sister.

But Daphne knew that Mrs. Havershall would not be satisfied until she had found out who she was.

CHAPTER FORTY-SIX

T he maid, Mary, was talkative the following evening as she took the pins out of Daphne's hair and undid her buttons at the back of her dress. She spoke of her brothers and sisters in Yorkshire.

"Do you 'ave brothers and sisters, Ma'am?" she asked then.

"I have one sister. My brother died when he was only five."

"Oh tha's very sad, ma'am. I'm sure your family must 'ave suffered a lot. What was 'is name?"

"Gabriel."

"Gabriel! He's an angel now. Angel Gabriel."

"And do you 'ave sisters, ma'am?"

Daphne thought she was being a little curious, but perhaps she was just friendly. Maybe she knew that she wasn't of this rank and felt at ease with her. In the adjoining room, she could hear Ethan lecture the footman about something.

"I have one sister, Rebecca. She's two years younger than me."

He said nothing, only looked again at the small, still white form in the cradle, dressed in one of the beautiful white gowns of linen and lace that she had lovingly sewn for him, with a bonnet.

"We'll try again." he muttered. Daphne shivered, shaking her head.

Over the next several days, during her lying-in, her labour replayed itself over and over in her head like a recurring nightmare. She never wanted to go through that again. Ever!

When the doctor visited she told him so.

"Oh come now, you're not eighteen yet, are you? You're not even grown, Mrs. Webster! In my professional opinion a young woman is not physically ready to bear a child until she is past eighteen years old. But this fad for early marriage – you should have waited and not been in such a hurry to shake off the spinster state! However, the outcome is nobody's fault, not yours, not mine. These things happen. And allow me to reassure you, in case this is on your mind, that your second labour will be nothing like this one. You'll sail through it."

"Is that true?" she brightened up. "I was going to tell my husband I never wanted to have to bear another!"

"For shame, Mrs. Webster! You can't keep your husband from you like that! You'll have six bonnie babies or more, if I'm not mistaken. Well, I shall expect to see you next year, Mrs. Webster, and never fear! Never fear!"

"So she's at 'ome with your parents, then?"

"No, my father died when we were young." Daphne said no more. She did not know what to say of her mother.

The following day, a walk was planned, a tour of the Park, and a climb to a small hillock from where there was a lovely view of the country. Daphne kept well away from Mrs. Havershall. Lady Ellen had taken a great liking to her and bade her walk by her side. She pointed out various objects of interest as they walked along. The men had gone riding. Besides Lady Ellen in their group, there was a Mrs. Hitchens and Mrs. Fenwick-Jones, both young women like herself. They would have ignored me, she thought, if Lady Ellen wasn't so nice to me. Daphne did not speak much to anybody, remembering Ethan's words.

The following day, the women went riding with the gentlemen, but Daphne, never having been seated on a horse, had to refuse. To her dismay, she was left in the sole company of the woman she most wished to avoid. Mrs. Havershall did not ride either.

They were in the library, one of the largest and most comfortable rooms in the house. It was a well-lit room filled with cosy nooks, with sofas and high-backed leather chairs facing in all directions. Mrs. Havershall had invited Mrs. Webster to come and see it, and she rang the bell and told the parlour maid to bring them tea there.

Daphne was thinking of pleading a headache and going to bed after the tea, wondering if it would be very rude, but when the maid left the room, Mrs. Havershall said:

"Well, Mrs. Webster. I think I know who you are. I'm not terribly sure, so please excuse me if I am wrong. I think your maiden name is Swansea? I apologise, if I have spoken out of turn, and will say no more, if you tell me I am quite wrong."

Daphne realised that Mrs. Havershall had provided her with a way out if she did not wish to be identified, and this act of charity made her soften towards her. What harm would it do? Ethan, she knew, would be furious, but this lady had meant something to her family once, and she warmed to her.

"You're right, Mrs. Havershall," she said with a faint smile. "I am Daphne. But how perceptive you are. I have changed a great deal since I was eleven years old!"

"You have grown up into a pretty young woman. As for my perception – I cannot claim credit for that. I asked my maid to ask yours about you. She knew your name was Daphne, from your husband, and then last night, she learned about little Gabriel. I only knew one little boy named Gabriel, and that was Gabriel Swansea. Poor dear little boy! I did so love him!"

"We all did..." Daphne said softly, her eyes moistening.

"How did it happen, Daphne?"

She hesitated a moment.

"Do I have your confidence, Mrs. Havershall? Our story isn't pleasant. I wouldn't wish it known – "

"It's safe with me, Daphne. I might be an annoying sort of person, but I can keep a confidence."

"We had to move to Blossom Meadow, you know – almost the worst place in Manchester - to the most foetid and horrid room you can imagine, and Gabriel became ill there with cholera. He was gone in a matter of hours."

"Good gracious, child! How tragic! Blossom Meadow! Oh how did you sink so far as to have to move there?"

Daphne saw no reason not to relate all that had happened to them, including the sorry state that her mother had come to, how hopeless it all was, how her remarriage had improved their situation, but how she had begun to drink and gamble again and how she had disappeared.

Mrs. Havershall held her head in her hands. "You do not know how many times I have lain awake berating myself for forcing that spirit upon her. I often wondered how she was getting on, but she had made it so clear that she wanted nothing to do with me, that I never went back, never made any enquiry about her or any of you."

"It was not your fault," Daphne said. "You believed you were going to do her good. You didn't know how strong this weakness is, in her family. I will never touch any. I don't know about Becky."

"But you have done well, Daphne. You captured the heart of Mr. Ethan Webster! I admit I am not acquainted with the family, but he seems like an amiable young man. What is his profession?"

"His father owns Webster Cotton, which he is heir to."

"Well done, Daphne!"

"Please don't say that, Mrs. Havershall. Shall we take a walk in the grounds now, if you don't mind?" The headache that Daphne was thinking of inventing for herself had become a reality, and she needed fresh air.

They walked out into the Park, and by the little lake with the ducks and Daphne confided all – her forced marriage, the loss of her child, and how horribly she was treated by her in-laws, even by her husband. What did it matter? She had no friend, no confidante, and the burdens had weighed very heavily on her heart for a long time. She talked and talked and talked. She mentioned her great fear of another childbirth, for the doctor's words had not reassured her, and she was in the family way again, she was sure of it.

"But he was right, my dear. The first one is dreadful for most women, but was particularly horrible for you. But next time, get a doctor who will give you chloroform. I know of one. A Dr. Marshall. A wonderful woman's doctor; my daughter-in-law swears by him, and she's had four! And you shall have rosemary tea as a tonic on your next, not to be taken until you are near confinement; mind you, that is very important. And when you are in labour, have something to eat, whatever you fancy, no matter what the doctor says, you need strength at the end. I always had bread and honey."

Daphne chuckled to herself in spite of all the pain that re-opening her wounds had inflicted upon her. Mrs. Havershall was just the same, and it was reassuring, and reminded her of happier times when she used to visit, sit in the parlour, and advise her mother about everything. Why had everything changed?

They never noticed the face peering at them from the library window. It was half-amused, half-contemptuous. Mr. Fenwick-Jones had been too lazy to go out riding, and had instead gone to the Library and stretched out on a sofa facing one of the bookcases. When the ladies had come in, he'd thought of declaring his presence, but the conversation took a very interesting turn indeed, and he'd heard the whole history of Mrs Webster and her mother Mrs. Swansea drowned in drink; their removal to Blossom Meadow; the unsuspecting Mr. Byrd; all ending with Mrs. Byrd running away with a lover, having ruined him! It occurred to him that he should not divulge anything, but this was too good an opportunity for a lark with his friends! He chased away the still, small voice of his conscience, put Gabriel out of his head. Tragedy would take the amusement out of his story, and he gave himself over wholly to the temptation to gossip. How could he possibly keep this to himself? It was magnificent!

CHAPTER FORTY-SEVEN

Mr. Fenwick-Jones regaled his friends the following morning, and all were fascinated and amused, with one exception – Lord Longstone. He thought it was a most unfortunate story that should not have been repeated, and Fenwick-Jones was quite offended at Longstone, and considered leaving. But the cat was out of the bag and within hours, Ethan was playing billiards with Hitchens, found himself at the butt of a joke.

"We hear that your lovely wife gets her fine bloom from a place she once lived, is that so?" Hitchens shot the ball expertly at a bunch of balls in the middle of the table.

"What do you mean?" Ethan was genuinely puzzled.

"A Meadow full of Blooms or - Blossoms, perhaps?"

So that was his meaning! It was a rather lame attempt at an insult, but it was an insult.

"I do not know what you're getting at, Hitchens." Ethan shot badly, and the ball only grazed the ball he had taken aim at.

"Feather shot! Oh come now. Her mother sunk deep into debt, and had to move there, then she became a noted success at the crap table, and left her old husband to abscond with the croupier!"

The tale had become embellished with every hour.

"Where is she now, Webster? Earning a fortune in Monte Carlo? You have interesting relations."

"Excuse me," said Ethan, laying down his cue, though he wished to lay it about the man. "I have some urgent business to attend to."

It was about five o'clock when Daphne came up to the room to change for dinner, and found Ethan packing his clothes.

"What are you doing?"

"We have to leave now."

"Why? What's happened? Is your father ill?"

"No, but they know. Did you tell anybody? Because they know. Hitchens just gave me a history of your family. Where did he get it?"

She was stricken with shock and distress.

"Did you tell anybody?" he asked angrily, slamming the lid of his trunk.

"Mrs. Havershall recognised me." she said, in a low voice.

"Go and pack. Don't wait for the maid. I took leave of Longstone. He tried to dissuade me but I said I had urgent business in Manchester. What are you waiting for? Go!"

In the carriage, the words came out. Who Mrs. Havershall was and how she had confided in her.

"You're so naïve, Daphne. She went off and told everybody. This is the ruination of everything; I wish we had not come at all!"

The Webster sisters were very surprised to see them back, and Lavinia quietly triumphant and very gleeful because of the reason. Nothing could have pleased her more than to have her sister-in-law exposed as a fraud, even though it meant that her family would be disgraced with anybody who mattered. Mr. Webster was understanding and tried to take Daphne's side when he saw that even her husband was cross with her. As for Daphne, she was too miserable to care what they thought. Mrs. Havershall had betrayed her confidence. She had no friends, nobody in the world cared about her.

CHAPTER FORTY-EIGHT

Mrs. Havershall was very disturbed to see that the Webster's had gone home. She was sure it had something to do with the conversation that they had had. Had Daphne been distressed and regretful at having confided in her and persuaded her husband to take her home?

Lord Longstone found out that Hitchens had joked with Webster about his wife, and thought it very bad form. The Longstones were an old family, and were inclined to despise the snobbishness of the newly rich, like Hitchens, who had made their money from the importation of guana, a trade perhaps involving illegal slave labour. Lady Ellen was aghast when she heard. That poor little thing, what a struggle she'd had! No wonder she was so shy and reserved. Lady Ellen never met anybody before from such a notorious area of the city. A slum was as far away from her world as the moon. Mrs. Webster was a very sweet person. Lady Ellen had somehow during her upbringing formed the impression that the poor were all rough-spoken and criminal, oh, how wrong that must be! Mrs. Webster – Daphne - was a gentle woman, and she'd really taken to her; having a sincerity about her that was so lacking in many people she knew.

Lady Longstone recalled Mrs. Havershall telling her about a family she used to visit some years ago. A maid she had taken a great liking to, who'd had a very hard life. And that was one of the daughters, how interesting that was! How well she had done for herself, she was sorry now she had not taken more notice of Mrs. Webster, and observed her more keenly than she had.

But why had they run away, she mused to herself. Had she stolen something? She must ask Mrs. Beets to check all the valuables about the house and especially the rooms the Webster's had occupied. She hoped, for Sophie Havershall's sake, that nothing was missing.

CHAPTER FORTY-NINE

Lavinia was determined to get rid of Daphne. She'd ruined her brother's life, he was cross and miserable. But he would never be free to marry again, unless Daphne would die, or if there was a scandal and a divorce.

The wish became stronger. Was not there any way to get rid of her? At first, she played with ideas in her mind, not taking them seriously, but the more this thought occupied her, the more shape they took. Soon, she could think of nothing else. She shut out all objection; her conscience was put away. Daphne had ruined her brother and their entire family. It was a just cause.

Perhaps Daphne had inherited her mother's weakness for alcohol. If she could get her to begin to drink perhaps? She'd become a sot, like her mother, and perhaps run away with a man, giving Ethan grounds for divorce. But Daphne did not drink. She had to be tricked into it, then! It would not be too difficult to put some of Cook's liquors – rum perhaps - into her tea in the evening. Lavinia always made the tea when the boiling water was sent up, and handed the teacups around at night. The small bottle could be hidden in her pocket and it would be an easy matter to dispense it – just a drop at first, then a few drops more...and more...

CHAPTER FIFTY

D aphne frowned at the tea. "There's something different about it tonight," she said a little timidly.

"I don't find anything different about it." said Lavinia, pretending to be insulted.

"It tastes as it always tastes." said Helena, sipping.

The following evening, Daphne drank it without comment. And the next. A few more drops of rum were added over the next few weeks. How long would it take for a weakness to manifest itself? She was growing impatient.

Then Daphne decided to have a second cup of tea at night.

"Allow me," said her sister-in-law, jumping up. It was not the tea Daphne needed, it was the rum!

Daphne wondered at her kindness; she was certainly showing her more attention than before. Lavinia was very pleased. The weakness was present! Now, to offer her a real glass of something – white wine perhaps? She could pass it off as a gooseberry cordial, sweetened and disguised, Daphne would never suspect.

At this stage, she had to confide in Helena, convincing her that it was the only way to save their brother from a hellish marriage. Helena's weak character soon accepted the plan, though she pointed out to Lavinia that Daphne did not know any other man except Ethan.

"Everything in its own time," said Lavinia with irritation.

"And she is *enceinte*! Won't her baby grow up a sot?"

Lavinia thought about this for a moment. But she was too steeped in her plans to care.

"Nonsense. How many women do we know who drank wine when they were expecting, and their children are normal?"

"I do so feel like a glass of cordial," said Lavinia one day as they sat in the porch, a small but pretty enclosed area, decorated with tall plants, with a little round mosaic table and chairs. "I have a wonderful recipe from Miss Gormiston – made with gooseberry - I've been dying to try. You add sugar of course, and cloves and a pinch of cinnamon. Shall I make a jug?"

It was one of those golden October days, the porch had captured the sun, and was warm. Helena, intrigued, assented, so Lavinia departed to the kitchen. Upon her way, she opened the cabinet and took a bottle of white wine from it. Cook was resting before preparing dinner, and it was an easy matter to get a jug, the sugar and spices.

"That's so refreshing, Lavinia," said Helena, pleased. "Let me have another glass. I do like it."

"Daphne, more for you too?"

"It's making me feel a little woozy or something," Daphne said, passing her hand over her eyes. "No, I shall have no more."

"Oh come on, Daffy." Lavinia poured some into her glass, filling it.

Daphne did not miss the nickname, and at first felt a little moved that Lavinia had used it. She had never been called Daffy by her before.

"I thought you did not like me, Lavinia," she began, after taking a few sips of her second glass. She greatly surprised herself. What had loosened her tongue?

"We found it hard to get used to you, and you to us, but we are very fond of you, why you're like our sister now – you are our sister!" said Lavinia. "Is she not our sister, Helena?"

"Of course she is our sister!" said Helena with a little too much enthusiasm.

"You put something in this." said Daphne, the wine doing away with indecision about speaking her thoughts. "Why?"

"Put something into it, indeed! It's gooseberry cordial! A small child could drink it."

"It doesn't taste like gooseberry!"

"The spices disguise the taste –"

"Why, Lavinia? I think I know what you are trying to do. If I'm correct, it's a very wicked thing to do! Evil and wicked!"

"How can you speak like that to Livvy?" Helena cried.

"You're as bad as she!" Daphne put her glass down and flounced away. She went to her favourite spot, the pavilion in the back garden, where she sat down and leaned her head against a post. The red and gold leaves fluttered down around her and the lawn was covered in them.

She began to laugh. What had possessed her to say those things to Lavinia? She got up and did a little dance about the wooden floor. Then she realised suddenly what was affecting the change in her mood and in her manner. It was the alcohol – that thing she despised beyond all other things.

"Oh Mamma, "she said aloud. "It made *you* forget and it's making *me* brave!"

She returned to the house. The porch was empty, her sisters-in-law had gone off somewhere. But her glass was there, still half-full. She picked it up, looked at it, finished it and went upstairs to dress for dinner. By the time she came down an hour later, the effects had worn off and she saw, with a clear head, what had happened that afternoon. It was not good. This is what had happened to her mother. It had made her feel better, and she could not stop.

There would be wine at dinner. The servant, Giles, always went around the table and poured for everybody except Daphne.

They were seated. Mr. Webster said Grace. Giles came around the table with the bottle. She bit her lip as he approached to pass her by as usual to pour into Helena's glass – *'God help me,'* she prayed and held her breath as he passed, to stop herself from asking for some. He set the bottle on the table and left. They would help themselves after this.

She could hardly concentrate at dinner. The bottle fixed her eye. It seemed to call her. She did not answer its call, but felt sad and even a little angry that she could not. Why? She could not answer that.

Lavinia was unusually quiet and in bad humour. When the tea came later on in the drawing room, she handed Daphne her tea as she always did, sulking a little.

Her tea tasted different tonight. It lacked a little – kick. Then she remembered something curious. Cook, about six weeks before, had said that somebody had robbed a little bottle of liqueur from her pantry. She'd blamed the gardener, who had stormed off and almost gave notice. Daphne had told her to buy another and had not thought about it since. Now she wondered.

CHAPTER FIFTY-ONE

M rs. Havershall could not rest, her mind obsessed with what had happened to the unfortunate Mrs. Swansea – Mrs. Byrd, as she later became. Was she even alive? She visited every Temperance Hall in Manchester, for she could not think of anywhere else. She even enquired at the workhouses. Nobody had heard of Mrs. Amelia Byrd.

Her next thought was to place an advertisement in the newspapers; but Mr. Byrd might have something to say about that. She would have to see him.

"What?" he said, as she sat in his front parlour. "What business is it of yours, madam, may I ask? I don't want her found. If that rascal she ran away with has absconded I would have to maintain her again. No, the last thing I want is for her to turn up. Leave it alone."

"I wish to do it for Daphne's sake."

"Leave Daphne be. She's very happy and settled where she is. Bringing her mother back to her would cause her shame and disgrace. I go there for dinner every Sunday, and let me tell you she's happy as a pig in muck." He blew his nose hard.

Mrs. Havershall winced at the analogy, but Mr. Byrd was a rough man. She burned to tell him the truth; but dared not.

One day, while browsing the newspaper, she saw the following advertisement:

Retired police constable, still sharp in wits, seeks private employment. Specialties include solving robberies, finding stolen goods and missing persons. References available. Write to Crime Solver, at this newspaper. Reasonable terms.

Mrs. Havershall noted down the address, and wrote to *Crime Solver*. By return, she received an invitation to visit him at an address in Trafford. A little nervous about going by herself, she asked her son George to accompany her for protection.

"Mr. Albert Meek, retired from Manchester Police," the beefy man said, bowing, before installing himself behind the desk in his small office, on a chair that seemed too small for him, and taking a piece of notepaper and a quill he dipped in ink. "What can I do for you?"

Mrs. Havershall told her story while he took notes.

When she had finished, Mr. Meek looked thoughtful.

"The only lead you have, it seems, is that of Miss Becky, who is purported to have sailed for America. However if her original intention in leaving home was to seek her mother, I think it wise to check the passenger lists for that time period, from Liverpool – that is the likeliest port. Thankfully her name is Swansea, and not Smith or Jones. It should be easy to find out if she has sailed. Can you be more specific as to the time she might have emigrated?"

Mrs. Havershall knew she would have to consult Daphne for that, but she was troubled about it. On the other hand it would give her a chance to clear her own name, if Daphne blamed her for what had happened at Longstone.

Mr. Meek gave them his terms, and they seemed reasonable. He then went on, and spent a little too much time on his impeccable qualifications.

"I was a policeman for twenty years," he said, showing them his reference. "I injured my leg while chasing a criminal in Ancoats. The superintendent gave me a desk job, but I couldn't stand being cooped up, so I retired, and set myself up here. I'm fortunate that I am acquainted with every cracksman, spiv and fence in Manchester. Fenians too." He added as an afterthought. "My investigations have brought me all over England, to Ireland, France and to Monte Carlo."

"And your success?" asked George Havershall, who was of a cynical nature.

"I find more people than I do not find, as I have time the police do not have. However you'd be surprised how many people do not want to be found. You should be prepared for that possibility."

"I see," said Havershall, still cynical. "Well, Mother, what do you think?"

"I must see Daphne Webster again," she said.

CHAPTER FIFTY-TWO

"**M**rs. Havershall?" Daphne had mixed feelings about the lady in the drawing room awaiting her.

"My dear Daphne, you left Longstone in such a hurry, we had no time to say goodbye. At the outset I must tell you that I had nothing to do with how a certain matter came to be revealed to the company at Longstone."

"No?" Daphne motioned for her to be seated, and took a seat herself.

Mrs. Havershall told her how it had come about. Daphne was very relieved. Her face relaxed and she smiled.

"I am sorry I thought it must have been you," she said. "I'm so happy that it wasn't!"

"But that is not what brings me here," the older woman replied. "Though it is good to have the opportunity to straighten out that matter."

She related all to Daphne, who listened with wonder, if not astonishment.

"Why would you do this for us?" she cried out.

"Because I feel guilty about what happened with your mother, it must be rectified as far as I am able."

"My mother may be dead." Daphne lowered her head onto her breast. "Gin was her life, her reason to get up in the morning. I think about her all the time. Sometimes I'm angry with her, sometimes I feel only pity. No matter what, I will always love Mamma. But I wish I knew what became of her."

Mrs. Havershall told her about the detective. Daphne brightened up.

"It was sometime in 1861, from April or May, that Becky is supposed to have left England." she said.

"Is there anything else you can tell me about where your mother may have gone, Daphne? Or anything about the man she left with? Where did she meet him?"

"A gin palace, not far from where we lived. My stepfather mentioned *The Golden Grove*. I remember passing it one day and taking a look at it. I understand there were other places they frequented."

"Mr. Meek can search there to see if anybody remembers her. Is there anything else you can think of?"

Daphne shook her head.

"Well that will have to do for now. It's something to go on."

"Mrs. Havershall, thank you for taking an interest."

"You're welcome, dear. Is there anything you want?"

Daphne hesitated.

"It seems like a great deal to ask…but I never get away from this house. Or its occupants. If you could call upon me every now and then, perhaps we could go for a drive?"

"I will call upon you as often as you wish, Daphne. Fresh air and drives will do you good. We can go to the country."

"That's very kind of you, Ma'am, to take me out. I have enemies here."

"Surely that is too strong a word." the woman protested.

"Miss Webster tried everything she could to make me succumb to drink, like my mother. But I found her out."

"That is evil of her indeed. You know what it says in the Bible, dear. *Be ye therefore as wise as serpents and harmless as doves*."

CHAPTER FIFTY-THREE

The gentleman among the crowd of spectators at Doncaster Racecourse was poring over his race card, oblivious to anything around him, when a lady, passing by, stumbled against him, jostling him.

"Oh I am sorry, sir!" she gasped. He tipped his hat, not really aware than on his other side, he had brushed up against another person, a man, as the lady had lost her footing and jostled him. The race was beginning! Where was Swiftly By? By George, he was leading! Come on, come on! All around him were shouting, the excitement was tremendous, but the man's mood changed to one of chagrin as Swiftly By was overtaken by a roan named Mellow May, who easily reached the finish line ahead of all the other horses, Swiftly By not even placing. He sighed, turned away, and stuffed his card into his pocket. His hand expected to meet the hard leather of his wallet; instead it met thin air. He remembered the woman who had stumbled against him on his other side, and the man he had brushed against as he had been jostled! What-ho! A pair of thieves! He spied a policeman and made his way toward him.

"Here, Bob. See you in half-an-hour." Richard Montague handed over the wallet to his accomplice friend in the shelter of a tall fence screening them from view. Amelia was nowhere to be seen. She would take another route back and he would meet her later. He pulled his cap over his forehead and walked with nonchalance down the street, and after turning a few corners, he knew he was safe.

Amelia was walking in the opposite direction when she heard a man's shout. "That's her!" Somebody could not be speaking of her, could he? She kept walking, though her heart beat very fast, steeling herself not to run down the street. She heard running footsteps behind her. What to do now? Run? No, that would show guilt. The peeler was before her in a moment, blocking her.

"Excuse me, ma'am –"

"What's the matter?" she feigned shock. "What's wrong? Why are you stopping me?"

"That's the woman who jostled me! Her accomplice stole my wallet!" blustered the man, who had reached them.

Amelia looked at him in surprised recognition.

"I did stumble against you," she said. "Yes, I did, I am so very sorry – but steal? What are you talking about, sir? I did not steal from you!"

"Were you with anybody at the Racecourse?" asked the policeman.

"No, sir, I came on my own. I must admit I like a little flutter, but I don't like anybody to find out."

"What's your name?"

"Mary Jones." The moment she had said it, she regretted it.

"I see, Mary Jones. Mary Jones!" The policeman produced his rattle to summon help. "Who were you working with, Mary Jones? Who is the man who picked this man's pocket?"

Amelia froze in fear. Of the police – and of Richard Montague. She had grown to fear him, and wished to be away from him.

"Who is he? What's 'is name?" The constable grabbed the back of her collar. "You have to tell me, or I'll charge you with obstruction of Justice you'll get a few years in jail."

Amelia was thoroughly frightened now, especially as several other policemen were running to the assistance of the constable.

"It's Richard Montague! Richard Montague is his name!"

"Richard Montague. Not his real name, I bet. Describe this man."

"He's about five feet seven, has dark hair, blue eyes –"

"Scars, birthmarks, moles?" snapped the Constable.

"He has a scar on his left arm. He told me he got it as –"

"Address!"

"Address?"

"Yes, where is he staying? Where is he now? Markham, you ready with a pencil?"

"Yes sir."

"Where is Richard Montague staying? Come on, Miss!"

"I don't know!"

"You do know." The constable seemed to be able to see through her.

She could not stay him any longer. She gave him Richard Montague's address, and furthermore, when pressed, the place where she knew he was to meet 'Bob' to divide the money.

Three policeman took off at a brisk run.

"May I go now?" she asked, desperately.

"No, of course not. You're being charged with theft, *Miss Jones*. You're coming along with me to the station. But first, empty your pockets and I will 'ave a look in your reticule, there."

"You'll find nothing, sir." Amelia said. But her bravado, had it ever been in existence, was completely gone.

"What about my wallet, Constable? There was forty pounds and six shillings in it!" asked the gentleman.

"If they're on time, you'll get it back, most likely." said the constable. "You'll be one of the lucky ones."

CHAPTER FIFTY-FOUR

rrested! Mrs. Byrd could not believe it, as she sat on a bench in a cell together with a half-dozen other women, all awaiting questioning, or cooling their heels after being found drunk and disorderly. She had sunk so, so low. She leaned her head against the bars and closed her eyes, almost wishing that if she shut out the scenes around her, she could pretend she was somewhere else, pretend that the last weeks – months - had never happened.

A part of her felt relieved. As long as she'd had money, Dick was pleasant. After that had run out, he'd made her work for him as an accomplice. He'd withheld gin from her until she agreed. He had other women, but if she left him, where would she go?

She wanted a drink now. It was her painkiller. Whenever she had thoughts that caused her pain, she had taken a sip. Or two. Or more. By now, Richard would wonder where she was.

She thought of Charles. If he could see her now! Thank God he could not! Her girls! Poor Daffy, poor Becky – what a short straw they'd drawn with a mother like her! She was utterly lost now.

She was taken to a small room, with bare grey walls, a small barred window, a table and a few chairs. A grey-haired policeman sat behind the desk, tapping his fingertips on the table, as the young constable delivered her inside. The Inspector nodded at him to stay and note down all that was said.

"Now Mary Jones. Your real name, please."

"Amelia Byrd."

The Inspector looked up.

"Right. That was not too difficult, was it? Were you with the pickpocket today?"

"I was, sir," she whispered. Tears fell from her eyes.

Inspector Craddock was an experienced man who could tell crocodile tears from genuine tears, so he simply sighed.

"How did you come to this, Mrs. Byrd? Do you know you have come to be involved with one of the most notorious and ruthless criminals in the North of England?"

"No!" she said, with genuine horror. "Richard Montague!"

"His name is not Richard Montague. The man you know as Richard Montague was born Thomas Dyer. He is now in custody, as is the fence. We caught them red-handed with the wallet. I am prepared to be lenient, if you will co-operate with me." he added with more severity. "I want to know about Thomas Dyer's activities for as long as you have known him. Tell me everything you know."

"Sir," she gasped. "You see me now, and I'm a wreck of a woman. I was a happy wife and mother until I lost my husband in a dreadful fire, in the warehouse where he worked. He was a foreman there. He died to save somebody else! In Manchester, it was! I was Mrs. Swansea then. I went to pieces after he died. Nothing was the same. I had never touched drink, never – but after I was given some as medicine, by a well-meaning lady – well, you see me now, I would do anything for gin. I remarried, and had to leave because of my drinking and gamboling! My children are with my husband."

"Mrs. Byrd, tell me everything you know about Dyer. Turn Queen's evidence, and you will get a light sentence. We want to get this gang off the streets once and for all."

Amelia recovered herself and began to talk. After she had finished, and answered several questions truthfully, the Inspector motioned to the young constable to take her back to the cage.

The young constable had a gentle manner. He said not a word. As he locked the cage door and turned away, he threw her a curious glance. She supposed it was because she had been Richard Montague's mistress and therefore had notoriety. She noticed an ugly scar on his neck and wondered if he had been injured by a criminal.

CHAPTER FIFTY-FIVE

Amelia Byrd stood in the dock, her head bent low on her chest. She was a spectacle of fun to those in the Gallery and had never been so humiliated in her life. Near her, Richard Montague – or Dyer – and three friends, all of whom she had put in the dock – had been at times during the three-day trial sullen and at other times, defiant. She'd felt Dyer's stare upon her more than once today, but did not dare to meet his eyes.

The Jury filed in and took their seats.

"How do you find the defendant Thomas Dyer?" asked the Judge.

"Guilty, my Lord."

His fence's name was read out with the same verdict. And the two others.

Then that of Amelia Byrd's.

"Guilty, my Lord."

The Judge handed out the sentences. It was the fifth offence for Thomas Dyer.

"I hereby sentence you to ten years penal servitude."

Ten years! She knew he simmered with anger, though no sound came from him.

Five years for the others. Now, it was her turn. Oh please, God! Make him show mercy!

She had called on God a great deal in the last weeks, so she had admitted to herself that she did indeed believe in Him. She had knelt and asked pardon for her sins, and wept many tears since she had been arrested.

"Mrs. Byrd, I hereby sentence you to one year penal servitude."

Amelia took the sentence bravely. From the other prisoners on remand, she knew what penal servitude was. It was hard labour. Picking oakum or another dreary work devised as punishment.

"Where are we going?" hissed a young woman who looked very frightened as they were led off and put into a police wagon. She had been convicted of theft from a shop.

"No talking!" snapped a police matron.

"York Castle." murmured another prisoner, who knew the routine, when the noise of a carriage coming alongside them drowned out her voice.

York! As far away as that!

CHAPTER FIFTY-SIX

M rs. Havershall eagerly opened the letter from Liverpool.

'Dear Madam,

I have examined the shipping lists for April onwards, and there is nobody by the name of Swansea listed. Either Miss Becky changed her mind, or never intended to go at all. I also received your letter of the 6th in which you mention the Golden Grove Cheetham Hill. I will go there next. I would be pleased if you would let me have a remittance of five pounds by return for expenses.

Yours, Alfred Meek.

"I hope he can find out something worthwhile there." said Mrs. Havershall to her son. "Five pounds! I already gave him ten!"

Mr. Meek disguised himself as a labouring man about town, one who might frequent a gin palace, and entered the Golden Grove. It was an easy matter to strike up a conversation with the landlord and others nearby. Mrs. Byrd was remembered!

She took up with Richard Montague. Did he know that Montague was serving ten years in Yorkshire?

They knew nothing about Mrs. Byrd, but there was a girl – a girl come looking for her some time ago – said she was sixteen, which nobody believed. They'd sent her to a lodging house in Totten Square, where Montague played cards and recruited accomplices. Mr. Meek turned his steps there.

Another note went out to Mrs. Havershall, with another request for a remittance, which was granted, though with a request for an itemised account – which made him bristle. The end of the week found Mr. Meek in Doncaster. The entry of Richard Montague into the equation was a very lucky one; he merely had to look up the Assizes for the last several months. But no Richard Montague appeared there. His police background eased his way, and he was soon looking for Mr. Thomas Dyer. Ha! Here was the entry, he was sentenced to ten years for theft, and his accomplice, Mrs. Amelia Byrd, received one year and was transferred to York Castle.

He sat in his Hotel that evening and wrote to Mrs. Havershall.

CHAPTER FIFTY-SEVEN

"Oh this is so much worse than I expected," said Mrs. Havershall when she received the letter from Mr. Meek. "Prison! Poor unfortunate woman! She fell in with a bad lot. I don't think I should tell Daphne yet – in her condition, it might upset her greatly indeed. I heard of a poor expectant mother whose own mother fell and broke her foot in three places, and the daughter was so distraught at her mother's accident, that her baby was born with a toe missing–no, I shall not say a word."

"Oh Mother," her daughter-in-law Jennifer said. "That's just silly superstition! Modern doctors don't believe that sort of thing."

"Mother is afraid Mrs. Webster's baby will be born a criminal." said her son.

"You can laugh all you like, I shall not say a word to Daphne until after the baby arrives safely; she's worried enough as it is. Poor dear."

"You're not going to York, Mother, I hope." said Jennifer.

"Of course she is" said George. "Mother lives for her Causes. Don't you, Mother?"

"I only wish I could do the sleuthing myself" said his mother with spirit. "I must write to him, and tell him not to do anymore about Becky, for now. Look at this notepaper! The Reindeer Hotel! Why does he not stay in a room over a pub? I'm being fleeced! When I have been to see poor Mrs. Byrd, I'll decide where to take the matter."

CHAPTER FIFTY-EIGHT

The key rattled in the lock, the cell door opened and the warden appeared.

"Mrs. Byrd. A visitor for you."

Amelia was struck with apprehension. Was it her husband? Or one of her daughters? What would she say to them?

"Who is it?"

"How should I know?" said the warden crossly. "Come on, I 'aven't all day, 'ave I?"

But at least it was a diversion to follow the warden down the long hallway. New prisoners had to spend the first several weeks of their sentences largely alone to reflect and repent of their crimes. But she trembled at the thought of meeting somebody face-to-face, she was so ashamed.

She recognised Mrs. Havershall immediately.

"Amelia," said that lady. "I am so sorry to see you here, and before you speak, let me say, I blame myself."

Time had lessened Amelia's anger toward Mrs. Havershall, and she was truly glad to see her – a friend in this dreadful place.

"Don't blame yourself anymore. It was a time like no other. It's a long story, Mrs. Havershall."

"I know it all."

"How?"

Mrs. Havershall told her of her meetings with Daphne. It was news to Mrs. Byrd that Daphne was married, and had married so well! But she'd lost a child! Poor Daphne!

"Does she know of me being here?" she asked fearfully.

"No, and I won't tell her, unless you wish it."

"I don't wish it. What of my Becky? How is my little Becky?"

Amelia was distraught to hear that Becky was missing.

"She's full young to be out on her own. I needn't tell you the kinds of people I met, ma'am, on the streets. All sorts of criminals! Pimps! Thieves! And scuttlers! I'm so afraid for her, poor girl! I suppose her stepfather doesn't care at all about her. Will you tell him you found me?"

"No, actually – he does not want you found."

"Good. I should never have married him, I didn't love him, but was desperate. I stayed off the gin for a good long time, but – I needn't tell you I'm right ashamed of myself, now."

"Time's up!" snapped the warden.

Mrs. Havershall gave Mrs. Byrd some things for herself that she had brought. It had taken some research on her part to find out what a woman in prison wished for the most. A few pretty things went a long way to brighten up the life of a female prisoner. She gave her ribbons, combs, scented soaps and a good towel.

"I'm sorry we fell out." Amelia's eyes brimmed with tears. "I said horrible things!"

"We will not say another word about it." was the warm reply.

"One good thing about here, is that I'm off the drink, and ma'am, when it's nowhere around and I know it can't be got, I don't miss it. Maybe good will come out of this, I hope I can stay off it after I get out of prison."

"Time's up, I said!" the warden's voice was testy. Her eyes had popped at the luxuries bestowed upon the prisoner. Mrs. Byrd was due to be out of solitary confinement in a few weeks, and she hoped that the gifts wouldn't induce her back to drinking, as some of her fellow-prisoners might offer her spirits in exchange for one of those pretty soaps. They were not supposed to have it, but they had it smuggled in, and sometimes even wardens obliged, for a little remuneration.

Mrs. Havershall was passing through the gate of the prison to the outside, when she asked the guard stationed there:

"Excuse me, my good man, can you tell me what a scuttler is?"

He looked amused.

"He's a wild youth, roams the streets lookin' for trouble, beats up anybody who crosses 'im or if 'e imagines someone slights 'im. Scuttlers move around in gangs. They plague the police."

"And a pimp? What is a pimp?"

"That, ma'am, it ain't proper to explain that word to a lady. I'll just say this – a pimp sends women out to work for 'im, and takes their earnings." The guard gave a big wink, leaving Mrs. Havershall in no doubt as to his meaning.

"Gracious me!" she said, getting into her carriage. "I don't know anything about the world at all!" She wondered if she needed to continue the search for Becky, to save her from pimps and scuttlers. She had decided to do just that, when a letter from Mr. Meek at home informed her that he had urgent business in Town, and had to return there immediately, and had to postpone any other commissions she had for him.

"I can't say I'm sorry to lose him." Mrs. Havershall said.

CHAPTER FIFTY-NINE

"**D**o you need anything, love?" Ethan was tender in his care of Daphne. She was about to go through this ordeal again to give him a son. He knew she was deathly afraid.

"I have all I need, when you are good to me, Ethan."

"I think you're very brave. All women are very brave." He said warmly. Certainly his feelings for Daphne had softened since he learned that she was *enceinte* again. He sat on the side of the bed and stroked her cheek as she lay there, a ray of sunlight illuminating her wheaten hair. He was on his way to the Mill for the day.

Daphne caught his hand and pressed it to her cheek.

"You can be so loving sometimes."

"I'm not a bad man, you know." he said, a little peevishly, getting up. "See you this evening, then. Take care of yourself, and our son." he kissed her.

Daphne's maid came in with her breakfast. It was nice to eat without Lavinia and Helena.

A mill owner named Mr. Corbett had recently asked for Lavinia's hand, but Lavinia did not want him. She disliked his entire family, especially his mother with whom she would have to live, and she thought his younger sisters plain and haughty. Daphne had been disappointed. If Lavinia established herself elsewhere, Helena's good qualities could blossom. But under her older sister's influence Helena was well on her way to becoming just like her. Daphne heartily wished that Lavinia would fall in love.

CHAPTER SIXTY

Becky Swansea was tired from walking, so she sat on the banks of the River Don on a dry stone. She was utterly miserable.

It had been the stable lad, Leo's fault! She'd told him she was not supposed to have followers, and he had kept turning up at the kitchen door, wanting to see her. Then he'd gone to a fair and came back with a few ribbons for her. She had nothing pretty so she accepted them. She wore them on Sunday and Mrs. Parker had demanded where she got them from? Cook had told her. That had done it. *'No followers'* had been the rule, and she was out on her ear with a week's wages and no reference. She'd come back to Doncaster, walking mostly to spare her money.

She'd gone back to the doss-house she'd known before, hoping to see familiar faces, and there struck up a friendship with a girl much older than her. Maggie hawked old pans and kettles but never had two pennies to rub together. She was a good listener and had a motherly way. Becky had trusted her, even telling her yesterday she had a week's wages and her savings, and was wondering where she'd go next. But last night, Maggie had made her a cup of strong tea and she'd slept very deeply. When she woke, and felt for her purse underneath her pillow, it was gone. And so was Maggie. She was not to be found in her usual place of commerce, near the bridge along the Don; the other hawkers had not seen her.

What had Maggie given her? She still felt sleepy, and it was afternoon. Now, sitting on the riverbank, the sun going down, she did not know what she was going to do for the night. She didn't even have twopence for lodging, and had not eaten all day. She couldn't go back to the workhouse on Hexthorpe Lane, she was afraid that they would think she was immoral. Mrs. Parker said she was writing to Matron to complain about her and to get another maid.

There was one way she knew she could earn her supper and lodging, but she was very unwilling to do it.

She felt very sleepy. She supposed it was the drug that Maggie had given her and also hunger that made her feel like that. The waters below looked inviting. Perhaps she could just slip in? What would it matter? Who would care? She felt herself go limp, like a rag doll. Then, she began to slowly slip downwards...she rolled...she did not try to stop herself...it would soon be over...the water received her, and though she winced at the cold, she allowed herself to slip in and drift like a piece of straw. She went underneath, conscious that she was making ripples. She supposed they were very pretty ripples, viewed from a bank...

"Miss! Miss Swansea!"

She heard the call, very faintly, coming from the bank where she had been sitting.

"Miss! Miss Swansea! Hang on, I'm coming in!"

She was barely conscious of splashes, loud and big, and water thrashing about her, before she felt herself in a strong, firm grip. She did not fight him – she did not really want to die anyway. She allowed herself to be brought to the bank, where she spluttered for a bit, and then burst into a torrent of tears.

"I saw you on the riverbank," said the young policeman. "I was just comin' over to see if you were orright, and then I lost sight of you. I know who you are. You're Miss Swansea."

She looked up at him, astonished. She had seen him before, on the street where she lodged.

"I have been watchin' you for a while," he admitted. "But if you please, don't think badly of me for't. I was only concerned for your welfare. About ten days ago, while I was passin' the Old Farthing on my beat, you were coming along toward me, and I 'eard your name called by a drunken fellow from across the street. *Miss Swansea.*"

"I remember some fellow hailing me," said Becky. "I took no notice."

"I saw you turn your 'ead away and knew it was an unwelcome bit of attention. But Swansea is an unusual name, and it got my attention, because I'm from Manchester, and I knew Swanseas there."

"Oh, are you from Manchester?" she spluttered, as if he had come from heaven. She wanted to throw her arms about him.

"Let's get you 'ome and dry and I'll tell you more."

"I don't have a home! I'm lodgin' in The Old Farthing, but I 'ave no money now, so I can't go back there."

"I'll take you to my mother then. She'll be mighty glad to see you, Miss Swansea. Are you able to walk?"

She was, by hanging on to him. She looked up at him. A fair, fresh complexion, with honest eyes and an open expression. There was a scar on his neck.

They walked through the streets, ignoring the stares of the people who saw a drenched policeman assisting a soaking girl to walk along. They supposed rightly that he had saved her from some misfortune in the river, and some women called down blessings upon him. The constable lived in a street of terraced houses called Bentley Lane.

"Oh God 'elp us all!" cried his mother, when he brought her in. "What 'ave you got there, Jem? She's drenched 'ead to foot!"

"Her name is Swansea, and she's from Manchester." said the constable. "Look after 'er, Ma, will you? I 'ave to get changed out o' these wet things, and then I 'ave to go back to make a report and sign out."

"Swansea? This is -?"

But he was gone.

She was taken to a bedroom upstairs and there she stripped and dried herself off, then clad in a nightgown far too big and wide for her and with a blanket draped about her, she was shown to the fire. She stuck her cold feet out toward the fender. There was an aroma of broth. She shook and trembled and the old woman gave her a bowl of it.

"Why are you being so good to me?" asked Becky, her teeth chattering. "You seem to know who I am, but I don't know anybody in this part of the country!"

"Does the name Fountain mean anything to you?" asked the old woman, poking the fire under the kettle.

Becky thought for a moment.

"There are Fountains in Manchester." she began. "One of them…was in the fire at Smithfield, the one my father died in. My father saved 'im. Jem."

"Aye, that he did, God bless 'im, and may he enjoy 'is reward! The boy 'e saved is my son! The man who took you from the river! Tha's Jem!"

"The constable?"

"The very same, child! He was fourteen years old then. He left the mill after that, and we came to live 'ere, where I have family. We've often wondered about you, your Ma in partickler. Jem joined the police last year. It doesn't pay much but it's regular. Did you see that scar on his neck? That was from the fire. Ah! Here 'e is back now."

"You're lookin' better." Jem said kindly, as he took his place at the table. His mother set a supper of broth, bacon and bread and tea in front of him.

Becky felt happy to be in from the cold, to be fed and to spend the night with these kind people. She cupped her warm bowl with her hands to warm them.

Jem explained more in between taking hearty bites of his supper.

"As I said, I 'eard your name called, so I 'ad a good look at you, no offence. I saw you go into the Old Fountain, and later that day I made enquiries, and found that you were a Mancunian and then I was more sure. They said you were in Doncaster looking for your mother. You see, Miss Swansea –" he hesitated a little. "I met your mother some time ago."

"You met Mamma! So is she here, in Doncaster? How is she?" Becky sat up, her eyes bright.

"She is well, but – I hate to tell you this, she's in prison in York. She got mixed up with a very bad lot, and was sentenced to a year for being an accomplice to theft."

Becky turned her head and burst into tears.

"There, there!" soothed Mrs. Fountain. "It's not all bad. Jem 'ere 'ad entire story, as she told it to his Inspector, about how she came to be in trouble! Look on bright side! She's off the drink in there you know, and she'll be out afore you know it. Here, luv, give me your bowl, and take a hanky. An' sit yerself up to table, for tea and vittles. Are you the older or the younger Miss Swansea?"

"I'm the younger – Rebecca. Everybody calls me Becky. At least I know that Mamma's alive and safe," snivelled Becky, blowing her nose.

"Jem came 'ome and told me that he thought you might be the same Swansea as we knowed in Manchester. I wanted him to approach you directly and ask you, but he was afeard you would get scared and run off. Lots of people do, you know, when they are approached by constables, though why I don't know, they are there to 'elp the public."

"Maybe you thought I was thieving," said Becky, half-smiling, taking her place at the table, while Mrs. Fountain poured hot tea into a cup. Jem looked a bit embarrassed.

"I thought I'd keep an eye on you from a distance." he said. "You seemed to be orright, though I did see you in company with that Julia Wilkins, who is a known thief."

"Julia Wilkins! I don't know anybody of that name. I was friends with Maggie Wall." Becky said, buttering a roll of warm bread.

"The very same woman, Miss Swansea. She has several aliases. But come to today, when I saw you on my beat, I was worrit about you – you seemed different, staggerin' a bit – I hoped you hadn't been imbibing."

"Maggie – Julia - drugged me last night and robbed me. No, I don't touch drink. I never will."

"I followed you to riverbank, watched you sat there, and just as I was about to come up and ask you if you were orright, and per'aps introduce myself, you were rolling down slope toward river. Was I alarmed, I can tell you, Miss!"

"It was so good of you to come in after me," Becky said. "I didn't know what I was doing, really. Whatever it was Maggie gave me was affecting my judgement, and I was weak with hunger."

"I don't know if you know this, Becky, but when Ma called to your house, after your father died, she was turned away – "

"Jem, there's no need –"

"It's all right, Mrs. Fountain. My Ma was very ill after Papa died. She went downhill as you know."

"I understood why she din't want to see me. I felt her pain, for I lost my own husband when Jem was a boy. I hope, when she comes out of prison, that she knows she'll have a home with me, if she wants it."

Jem looked a little dubious at this offer; for him to live with an ex-convict would not be something he would want his Chief to discover; however, there was ample time to think about that. For now, he was happy to repay the debt owed by his family to the Swanseas.

"I'm making up a bed for you upstairs, Becky." said Mrs. Fountain, busying herself with sheets and blankets she took out of a cupboard beside the fire. "I'm right happy you're safe an' well. I told you, Jem, not to delay making yourself known! Becky wouldn't 'ave done a runner if a nice policeman 'ad a-spoken to her, would you dear?"

"Oh Mother, you don't understand how it is out there in the world." sighed Jem, with a wry smile towards Becky, as he drained his cup. "I'll look fer Julia Wilkins, to get yer money back, Miss Becky, but I'd say she's done a runner someplace."

Becky got into bed a little while later – and suddenly, remembering something important, got out again. She had not done this for years, but now she knelt by her bedside, and clasped her hands.

"Oh God, I know now you're there – my life is a gift, and if there's a gift, well somebody 'ad to give it to me – it is You. I found my Mamma and she's safe. That's a gift too. I'm sorry I din't try to save myself, when I felt myself slipping down to the water – someone somewhere must be praying for me. Please bless that someone."

CHAPTER SIXTY-ONE

There were two 'someones' praying for Becky. Daphne and her mother. Amelia who now having a heart more tranquil than she had had in years, and having ample time to think, reflected on her life, using the times when she and her fellow-prisoners were under orders of strict silence in the hours of work. Her aim was to be strong enough in faith when she was released, to be able to resist the temptation to drink again, for she knew it would come. It had done her, and her children, and her husband, great harm! She prayed for Daphne also, for though Mrs. Havershall had not directly said, she felt that Daphne, for all her money and position, was lonely and unhappy.

Then one day, she had a long, long letter from Becky! Her heart sang! She read it over and over again, and wept. The Fountains, of all people, to take her in! And Becky – Becky had come all the way to York!

As soon as I heard you were in York, Mamma, I looked in the Gazette, but I had no references. Mr. Fountain went in his uniform all the way to Mrs. Parker and told her I had been very badly done by and told her she had better write me a reference, and he frightened her enough that she did it there and then. So I was accepted by a good family and Mamma, when I look out my attic window I see the women's prison and I know I'm near to you. I will visit as soon as I can.

Mrs. Havershall wrote also. Daphne was nearing her confinement. She would let her know immediately how it went. When the baby was born, did she have permission then to tell her that her mother was safe and well?

While Amelia picked oakum, digging her fingers in to pull the tough strands apart, she tried not to think of what she was doing, but of something more pleasant. Her courtship days with Charles. Her wedding day; her babies coming. The happiest part of her and her children's day, when Charles came home from work – a golden glow bathed all her memories of that time. Often, it was hard not to dwell also on the bad memories. They were there in plenty also, but by now every woman knew her misfortunes, and Amelia knew everybody's misfortunes also. A few of the women had spirits smuggled in; she avoided them.

She wrote Becky a warm, optimistic letter. She urged her to write to Daphne if she had not already done so, but on no account was she to tell Daphne that she was found, because then she would have to say that she was in prison. This was the rule until Daphne's baby was born.

Becky read the letter with as much astonishment as her mother had felt on receiving hers. It was the first knowledge *she* had that Daphne was married, and into the Webster family of all families! So that's why she never answered her letters – she'd never even received them! The Whisker had of course thrown them away!

CHAPTER SIXTY-TWO

Daphne was still enjoying the tender attentions of her husband, and she was sure that they had turned a corner. Christmas was happy, and a surprise letter in the post brought a letter from Becky! She was in York, not America, and she had written letters already which she had never received. York! Not America! Apart from sharing the letter with Mrs. Havershall, she kept the information to herself, for nobody was interested in anything her own family was doing. Becky did not even mention their mother, which troubled her, as her purpose in leaving home had been to search for her.

Early one morning in February, her pains came. She woke Ethan, and he saddled his horse and went for the doctor immediately. Kitty was roused from sleep and lit a blazing fire and made her a cup of tea and brought her warmed bread and honey.

Even before the doctor arrived, Daphne felt that this labour was different. She was very happy when Dr Marshall said she was progressing very well – the pains, though intense, were hurrying her along, unlike the last time, and this gave her confidence that all would be well this time.

Just before ten o'clock the cry of a newborn babe came from the room upstairs, causing ripples of delight and relief to spread through the entire household.

"He lives! The child lives!" cried Ethan, springing up from a chair in the drawing room.

"God be praised, all is well!" said his father.

"We are aunts at last!" cried Helena to Lavinia. "I am Aunt Helena! How I shall love being an auntie! I shall spoil him!"

"I hope she doesn't want to name him after her dead father," was Lavinia's acid contribution. "*You* should be given that honour, Papa."

Giles was in the pantry polishing silver, and he smiled from ear to ear when he heard the newborn's wail. Mrs. Webster had done her duty this time – but only if it was a boy.

"Thank God!" cried Cook when told the news by the housemaid, Kitty, who dropped her duster in the morning room and ran down to tell her. "I do 'ope the poor Mistress is all right. Maybe they'll be nicer to her now."

Outside, tending some early blooms, the gardener heard the cry and smiled up at the window. William, the groom, was also informed by Kitty, who had a secret hope of presenting William with a child someday in the misty future.

Inside the house, Ethan took the stairs in long strides. His son was born and was living!

He knocked on the door, and was admitted straight away.

"Congratulations, Mr. Ethan." said the doctor. "You have a beautiful, healthy daughter."

A daughter? A girl?

His face fell as he brushed past the doctor and came to Daphne.

"It's a girl." he said stupidly.

"I know – isn't she pretty?"

Ethan looked down at the red-faced crying infant in Daphne's arms.

"Oh, darling, look, there's your Papa!"

"You've given me a girl."

It was an accusation and the delight faded from Daphne's face.

"Ethan." she said, looking up. "Go away."

He turned and walked away.

CHAPTER SIXTY-THREE

Over the next few days, Daphne enjoyed her new motherhood, and refused to allow Ethan's reaction to affect her mood. She loved their baby, even if he did not. She blocked him from her mind. But like a small seed, an idea was growing and growing within her mind. She did nothing to check it.

She had had enough of this house. She'd had enough of this family. She'd had enough of Ethan Webster.

She was going to take her little babe away as soon as she could, and make a life for both of them somewhere else.

There had been no discussion about a name for a girl. So she named her Amelia Honoria, after her two grandmothers.

Helena doted on the baby; Lavinia looked on the child with some cynicism – Daphne had not done her duty and borne the Webster Empire (or so Lavinia called the mill) a son and heir. She was utterly sympathetic to her brother.

If Ethan was in any danger of getting over his disappointment and becoming fond of his daughter, and of becoming more loving toward his wife, Lavinia kept reminding him of his misfortune.

"It is truly dreadful, even if she ever has another. It may be a girl again! Look at the Holmes'. Six girls! Poor Mrs. Holmes is old before her time, she looks about sixty. And how embarrassing for Mr. Holmes, having to admit to everybody that he has no son to inherit. I do hope Daphne does not have girl after girl."

One time when Ethan said, rather brightly – "Daphne is quite a plucky little woman, really, isn't she? And the baby is a pretty little one. I'm taking the carriage into town to buy them presents. Can you suggest anything?"

"Really, Ethan. Don't spoil her. Leave that to Helena and me. Women know better what a woman and child need. Also, it's not very seemly for a man to keep going into the nursery to see his child. The servants will laugh at you! And Daphne does not want to see you all the time. She's lying-in and needs to rest."

Ethan, having a weak mind, was swayed by Lavinia's opinion.

"Who is this?" asked Helena, looking out the window at a carriage coming up the avenue.

"It must that interfering old woman!" Lavinia said with disgust. "I think we should turn her away, Helena, don't you?"

"Daphne is rather fond of her," said Ethan. "Let her see her."

"Oh, as you say. You're her husband. But keep her away from me, I can't stand Mrs. Havershall. Go out to the hall, Helena, and ask Kitty to show her straight upstairs."

CHAPTER SIXTY-FOUR

Daphne nearly cried when she saw Mrs. Havershall.

"Please," she said, almost at once, clutching her arm as the woman bent to admire the baby. "Take me with you when you leave. I'd much rather be in your house than this one. Ethan is angry because I had a girl child. I can't bear it anymore. If you don't take me away with you, I shall take the infant and slip away by myself."

Mrs. Havershall plunked down on a bedside chair.

"Daphne, Daphne, don't upset yourself, it will affect your milk! You are nursing the baby yourself, are you not? Good! No spicy foods or cabbage, mind. Oh, what a sweet little darling! Does she cry a lot? Put her on her tummy. No pillow – she is far too young! Oh, my dear girl, you need a mother with you to teach you – there – I have a wonderful idea! That will be our excuse! You shall come away with me today. I shall convince them that you need me. Call Kitty to get you dressed and ready, and wrap the baby up very warm. I shall go downstairs and tell them you are coming with me."

In spite of Lavinia's resolve not to see Mrs. Havershall, she was forced to entertain a lecture from her on why Mrs. Webster should move to Havershall Hall that very day. Ethan seemed astonished. He could not understand why Mrs. Havershall looked upon him with disdain.

Mr. Webster's carriage drew up just as Mrs. Havershall was ushering Daphne and her baby out the front door. An explanation followed – Mr. Webster reluctantly agreed that it was the right thing, if Daphne needed help, that an experienced matron should deliver it. But would Mrs. Havershall not like to come and stay, instead of Daphne moving on this cold day to Havershall Hall? No, it was not to be thought of, Daphne said. Something in the way she said it, and the sudden tears that came into her eyes, startled him.

As the Havershall carriage rattled down the avenue, Lavinia remarked: "She cannot even take care of her own infant! What a ninny."

"That's enough, Lavinia." said her father. "I don't think I have ever heard you say anything nice about your sister-in-law. When Daphne returns here, I want you all to give her the respect she is entitled to. Do you hear me?"

Daphne settled in very comfortably at Havershall Hall. She had a pretty and cosy room with a blazing fire. She very much appreciated that Mrs. Havershall, though overbearing and bossy, was a truly caring woman who loved the Swansea family. If only her mother could know it too! Whatever had become of her?

She had made up her mind that she would never return to Victoria Park. Perhaps it would not be wise to tell Mrs. Havershall that. She would be reminded of her duty to go back and conceive a boy child. When she wondered briefly if she should go back, the memory of Ethan's face when the doctor had announced a daughter flooded her mind. It made her angry and hurt on her baby's behalf that he did not love his daughter immediately! Angry and hurt on her own behalf that he had said *'You've given me a girl'* and angry and hurt that his visits after the birth had been rare.

Ethan did not care for her. He never had. Nobody in that house cared for her. Mr. Webster, perhaps, but he was out most of the time and did not see how she was treated by the others. She felt utterly at peace to be away from them all.

"My little Amelia," she said, taking the baby up and kissing her. "It will be just you and me, but we'll manage, won't we? You are the most precious baby in the whole world!"

CHAPTER SIXTY-FIVE

Mrs. Havershall wrote to Mrs. Byrd to give her the good news of mother and baby, and that the child was to be named Amelia, which she knew would please her very much. '*She is staying with me for her lying-in. It might be better to keep the news that you are in prison from her for just a little longer. I am afraid it might affect her milk.*'

Mrs. Havershall's grandchildren loved the new baby in the house, and the youngest, three years old, could not properly pronounce 'Amelia' so called her 'Emmy.' The name stuck.

Her in-laws paid her a visit after a week. She was polite but distant with them. Ethan wished to linger a little while with her alone, but Lavinia's sharp voice intervened.

"It's getting dark, Ethan, and there's a sharp frost."

Ethan kissed Daphne, then bent to kiss the baby.

Lavinia admonished him again. "Don't do that, Ethan. You will give her a disease. You should never kiss a baby." She gave Daphne a fiery look.

"Come back soon," whispered Ethan, pressing her hand. "I miss you."

No, I shall never come back, Ethan. You've hurt me too many times. If I had an opportunity to speak with you alone, I would tell you that without Lavinia, we might have a chance. But with her? None. She doesn't want to marry, and I don't want to live in the same house as she. No.

When Emmy was two weeks old, Daphne's lying-in came to an end, and she began to take meals with the family downstairs. She knew she was expected to return home, but did not dare to say that she had no intention of doing so. She laid her plans well.

Mrs. Havershall had given her a maid to attend her. Her name was Bridie. She was a cheerful and obliging girl, and Daphne enlisted her help to leave the Hall on the day that Mrs. Havershall and her daughter-in-law went to visit a friend. Bridie was engaged to be married to a groom on a nearby estate. He hired a hackney cab for her, and she said goodbye to Havershall Hall on a cold Saturday afternoon, asking to be driven to a hotel outside the City. The housekeeper tried to stop her from leaving, but could not.

Mrs. Havershall returned to find a letter handed to her by the agitated housekeeper.

Dear Mrs. Havershall,

I am sorry to leave you in this way, but if I were to do it in any other fashion, you would share the blame for my deserting my husband and in-laws. This way, you are innocent. I can't tell you where I'm going. But I have money. Please don't look for me. Thank you from the bottom of my heart for looking after me and little Emmy for the last two weeks. I am going far, far away, but do not worry – we will be in excellent hands.

I have written a longer letter to my husband and another to my father-in-law. That will explain all to them, and will completely absolve you of anything to do with my going away.

Yours sincerely,

Daphne Webster

CHAPTER SIXTY-SIX

"What is the meaning of this?" Mr. Webster stood in the hall, clutching a letter over his head, and bellowed through the entire house. "What is this? Ethan! Lavinia! Helena! Come here, all of you! Do you hear me? All of you! Now, this instant!"

They came from different parts of the house to him. Ethan came also holding a letter in his hand, his face white.

"The drawing room." He led the way in there, and slammed the door shut after they had assembled.

"What is this, Father?" Lavinia asked.

He looked about at them all, from face to face.

"Sit down. I have a letter to read to you. Then you shall have a chance to defend yourselves."

Dear Father-in-law,

I write in sorrow. I find I cannot return to your home. I have been treated so badly, and with such cruelty, since I entered your house as Ethan's bride, that I must go. Lavinia in particular has been very cruel. She gave me no help when I arrived, deliberately humiliated me, in front of the servants as I tried to learn about running a large household. Helena might have a good heart, but she is so easily led by Lavinia, who makes sure nobody likes me. Lavinia even tried to send me down the same path as my unfortunate mother by tricking me into drinking wine and spirits. Lavinia has even undermined me to my own husband. I have written to him separately. I cannot endure this mental cruelty any longer! I have suffered so much under your roof, and refuse to raise my child – my beautiful, healthy child whose arrival occasioned disappointment instead of joy – in a home where she sees her own mother continually abused, and where the bad example of her aunts may influence her. I love her too much to expose her to those evil influences. Do not try to look for me. I have money, and for that I am grateful to Ethan, at least. I am going far away and will not be found. I wish you all well and happy. As we shall be in the future.

Helena was crying bitterly. Ethan had his head in his hands. Lavinia was looking about her, her eyes narrowed.

"Ethan, I shall speak to you privately, later. Lavinia, what have you got to say for yourself?"

"Of all the disgusting, cunning little liars, she is the worst!"

"Daphne is not lying!" cried Helena. "You wouldn't allow me to give her the housekeeping keys or to tell her she had to give Cook orders! And you slipped rum into her tea and tried to make her fond of wine! And you even hoped she would die in childbirth!"

Ethan looked up, shocked.

"Lavinia!" he said. "You hoped she would die? She went through a hellish experience, and came near death and you did not even say a prayer for her? How wicked of you!"

"And if she died, you'd be free to marry again, wouldn't you? Perhaps Lady Ellen or someone fitting to be mistress of this household? You would have shed tears but been secretly glad. You hypocrite!"

Her father raised his hands to put an end to the discussion. He turned towards his eldest daughter.

"Lavinia, you have one month to make an arrangement to leave this house for good. You accept Mr. Corbett or hire yourself out as a governess, or – work in my mill. On the factory floor, in your bare feet, living in poor lodgings. But I want to know your plan by the end of March."

"Father!" she said, leaping from her chair. But he was not paying attention.

"Helena! You may stay for now, until I see how you are without your sister's influence. I would like though, to see you involved in charity work instead of lounging around here all day reading one trashy novel after another. Yes, I know your tastes, girl. You shall pay a call on Mrs. Clements and ask to join Victoria Park Charitable Society, which as you probably know takes food, clothing and medicine to poor families. Now, girls, leave the room – there will be no argument – and I will speak to my son alone."

The girls got up and left, Lavinia white as death, her teeth clenched; Helena in floods of tears.

"Father –" began Ethan hotly after the door had shut behind them. "I have something to say before you start on me. You forced this marriage upon me. That was not right. Not for me, nor for Daphne. You and that vulgar man Byrd plotted it. He could not wait to be rid of her."

His father raised his hand in a hopeless gesture.

"Ethan, I now very much regret my action. I was wrong. Your mother and I thought that settling you down would make you grow into a man. But marriage cannot supply what is wanting in you. You're irresponsible, spoiled and pout like a child when you do not get your own way. You count blessings as curses, such as your healthy little child.

"From this day you are going to have to earn your inheritance. I am changing my will to leave every penny of the Webster fortune to various charities, except for a small allowance for all of you, for thirty pounds a year. I may – I may change it back again in one year, if I see any improvement in my children."

There was silence for a moment.

"But what do I have to do to get Daphne back?" said Ethan unhappily.

His father seemed surprised at his train of thought.

"Am I to understand then that you have an affection for her after all?"

"Oh yes, Father, but I'm full of flaws. She is so much better than me. I thought I was better than she, but she's the superior one! I want her back. When I thought she was dying upstairs, I was in a dreadful state – then when she recovered, I went back to my old ways. Now she's gone, and I regret what I have been. I don't deserve Daphne." He waved his letter. "She tells me things about myself that are truly hurtful. I am very indignant, but - I am guilty of them."

"There's hope for you, then. But for the next year, I want you to earn your own living. You must leave tomorrow, and do not return here for a year. You probably have some money on you, when that has run out, there is no more. There is no point in going to the bank – I will take your name from the account, and you cannot ask for credit at any of the shops where we have accounts. Do not look for work in any textile mill."

"Father, what shall I do? This is uncommonly cruel and unfair! These are hard times. And I only have about five shillings cash. Besides, I need money to look for my wife!"

Mr. Webster did not fully trust that Ethan truly wanted Daphne back. It could be a ruse to get out of having to earn his own living the hard way. A year would test him.

"I will search for Daphne, I promise you. I want her back as well as anybody. Go, make yourself ready, and leave after breakfast, on foot. Take one suitcase."

Ethan gave him one last, long stare, and left the room. Before he opened the door, he went to the little table with his wedding photograph in its silver frame, and took it up and looked at it with regret. He took it with him. He did not bang the door, which was perhaps a hopeful sign.

CHAPTER SIXTY-SEVEN

E than left the house as ordered the following morning, on foot, carrying a large carpet bag. He jingled five shillings and some change in his pocket. He had one thought – finding Daphne, and recovering her love.

Though she had said she was going far away, Ethan doubted it. She may have said that to throw them off the track. Who did she know outside Manchester? He turned his steps toward the railway station, and asked the station master, the ticket master, guards and porters if they had noticed a young woman with a small baby travel unaccompanied anywhere in the last few days. He showed them the photograph. None could recall, but then there were so many trains, and so many passengers.

He walked to the office of *The Manchester Guardian*. He wrote out an advertisement, threepence a line. The clerk looked at him when he read it. "Are you sure this is what you wish to put in?"

"I'm sure. And I want it to run for as long as five shillings will buy me." He slapped the two half-crowns on the counter.

To my wife Daphne, please come back. I love you. In the future, it will be just you and me, I promise. We'll begin again.

"Very well sir." The clerk looked at him as if he were a curious specimen.

Out on the streets again, he did not know what to do. He supposed he should look for work. But where? He had no references. His prospects were very limited indeed. There was no point in trying any business where a position, even that of a clerk, required trust. He could not apply to become a valet in any home, or a tutor in a home or in a school. He went through several options while he walked about Manchester's streets, and rejected them all, and then found he was getting hungry.

His father had an extreme way of solving problems. Ethan is sowing his wild oats – get Ethan married! Ethan had everything too easy – throw him on his own resources for a year!

'I hope this does not backfire on you, Father', he said bitterly as evening came and hunger gnawed.

He had no skills, no trade, nothing to recommend him except his good looks and his superior way of speaking. But perhaps he could be a reporter for a newspaper. Why did he not think of that when he was at the offices of *The Guardian* this morning? He hurried his steps back there and asked to see the editor.

"Sir, how can I help you?"

"Mr. Garrett, I was hoping that you would find a place for me in your office. I am down on my luck, and have spent my last five shillings on an advertisement placed only this morning in this newspaper. My wife, sir, after some bad treatment by my family, has run off with our child. I have exhausted all my resources."

He looked at him dubiously.

"I say, aren't you the son of Mr. Webster?"

Ethan nodded, getting rather red in the face. He had just told the editor that his family had treated his wife badly.

"My father had nothing to do with the bad treatment of my wife, sir."

"And you?"

Perhaps gossip had seeped out that young Mr. Ethan had sorely neglected his wife. The editor seemed to know something.

"I hope that your wife returns to you, Mr. Ethan, but I cannot offer you a position." He said, somewhat stiffly.

He then tried a bookshop, a saddler's, even a hardware shop – but the lack of a reference got him the door each time. He was very hungry now, and cross also.

It was coming on to nightfall and he decided that his best chance of eating lay in those areas where people ate very cheaply – the poorer areas of town. He travelled down narrow streets and the smell of cooking drifted from doorways and windows to his nostrils as he passed.

He passed a pawn-shop. Of course! He'd never been in one, and only had the vaguest idea of how they operated. The window held an astonishing assortment of goods from corsets to silver teapots to toys. He pushed the door open. A woman in a shawl was parting with two candlesticks. "A wedding present," she sighed. "But times are 'ard now."

The pawnbroker looked at him with curiousity. He was not the usual customer.

He pawned two shirts for two shillings. It was not enough, he felt, but he could not argue with the pawnbroker, who failed to see that the pearl buttons were of as much value as the shirts themselves. Two shillings would buy him a good dinner and lodging.

CHAPTER SIXTY-EIGHT

For the next few weeks Ethan met his expenses by pawning nearly everything he owned, until he only had the clothes on his back left, the wedding photograph in its frame, and his watch. He walked about Manchester hoping to glimpse Daphne, but in vain. He went to Mr. Byrd's home to enquire if she had been in touch with him.

"Your father asked me the same question," Daniel said testily. "What's wrong with ye? Let her go. She's an ungrateful wench like her mother and sister. I'm well-rid of them and so are you, that's my opinion."

In May, he remembered morosely that Daphne's birthday was in the middle of the month. He'd never even given her a birthday present, and did not know the exact date. Shame on you, Ethan, he scolded himself. He had her letter – her stinging letter in his shirt pocket - and read it often, and thought about it, running the last two years over in his mind.

Making his way back to town, he passed a restaurant where he had often dined. He swallowed his pride and went in the kitchen door. The manager, Mr. Fortune, knowing him well, was willing to give him a trial. He pawned his jacket to buy his uniform.

How hard he worked over the next weeks, and how fussy the diners were! He resented their barked orders and superior attitudes, until he reminded himself that he was probably getting his just deserts for treating not only Daphne badly, but many people who had been in service to him.

"Excuse me, my wife's meat is underdone," said a gentleman to him one evening. He was a regular customer, a Colonel Thompson.

"She did ask for it rare, sir." said Ethan.

"Not that rare," snapped the Colonel. Ethan took the plate and Chef cooked it a little more before he returned it to the table.

"Ah! Waiter!" called the Colonel a few minutes later. "My wife's meat is now overdone."

"Overdone, is it, madam?" Edgar felt a hint of impatience creep into his voice. "What would you like me to do with it now?"

"What do you mean, my man?" snapped Colonel Thompson.

"What am I to do, in the situation? We cannot uncook it again, can we?" Ethan asked.

The Colonel's face grew bright red and his eyes almost popped.

"Just who do you think you are to speak to my wife like that? Get me Mr. Fortune immediately!"

Ethan was forced to stand and listen to how the Colonel had never heard such insolence and impertinence in his entire life, to which he cast his eyes to the ceiling, causing Colonel Thompson to say that he would never darken the doors of this establishment again, unless this young upstart was sacked on the spot. The other patrons were listening, and Mr. Fortune dismissed him with a week's wages.

How helpless he was, without his father's wealth behind him!

CHAPTER SIXTY-NINE

S ummer heat came to Manchester. Ethan was now living in lodgings in which he had to share his room with other fellows, two or three per night. At least he could still afford a bed to himself.

His search for Daphne had no result. He wrote to his father, who wrote back telling him that he had had no good fortune either. His father was of the opinion that she had gone to Scotland, Wales or Ireland.

There came the day when Ethan had to take the photograph from the frame and pawn the frame. He rolled up the photograph carefully so as not to crease it. His watch was the last item to be pawned. Summer wore on, and he moved to even cheaper lodgings, and then cheaper still, until he found himself at a doss-house called the Blue Bird in Tupper Square. What a great comedown this was! Cooking herrings over the fire, making tea for himself, drinking from a chipped tin mug and eating bread out of his unwashed hands, and all in the lowest company! Sharing a hard bed with a fellow who snored and smelled! And fleas!

The other lodgers were very interested in Ethan.

"So you're a toff, why're you 'ere?" a fellow called Wigs Shelton asked him, in between mouthfuls of pease pudding he'd got at a nearby cook-shop. "You mun be a gambler?"

"Yes, a gambler." Ethan said. "A very unlucky gambler."

"That room out back is shut down this long time. Have you seen whatsisname, Dick Montague? He broke out of jail a few weeks ago."

"I don't know who this fellow Montague is," said Ethan. "Never met him in my life."

"You might know 'im under a different name. A woman put 'im in jail, after being caught at Doncaster Racecourse. Her name was Byrd. He's going to get 'er, 'e is, fer snitchin' on 'im."

"Byrd?" Ethan raised his eyebrows.

"Yes. She's still inside. York, they send the women."

"What was her Christian name?"

"Oh, I don't know. Hey, Syl! Wot was the Christian name of that Byrd lady that got Dick Montague locked up?"

"Amelia, it wor, Amelia."

"And he said he's going to get her? How?" asked Ethan, losing interest in his bread and herrings.

"How should I know, Guv'nor? He'll be waitin' for 'er though. Pass that salt back 'ere, O'Brien, you don't own it."

Amelia Byrd. Was it Daphne's mother who was in prison and who would be in danger when she came out? Did Daphne know her mother was locked up?

He'll be waitin' for 'er. He did not like thet sound of that. He must find out more.

Syl came to his side, gave him a flirty look, and sat by him.

"You're new," she purred. "You're respectable, not like the others. I like respectable." She shook her wrist, showing off a good bracelet. "That came from a gent. One of my regulars."

"I'm married." said Ethan, crisply.

"So what? So are all the gents, or nearly. Why does that make a difference?"

"I love my wife and I'm true to her." Ethan said, inadvertently patting the letter in his shirt pocket.

"Oh, you're no fun then. What are you doin' 'ere anyway? Where is this wife, that she can't look to you? Look at you, a gent with a dirty face and dirty clothes!" Syl flounced off.

CHAPTER SEVENTY

Perhaps the way to find Daphne and his child would be through her mother.

He went to the police station. At first they took no notice of this man in shabby, dirty clothes, and when they did grant him an interview, told him to look sharp, they were busy. As soon as he opened his mouth, however, they took more interest in him. But Mrs. Byrd was not on any record they had. When he mentioned Richard or Dick Montague, though, they became animated. They were on the lookout for Richard Montague, or Dyer, was his real name, who was on the run. They gave him a description.

"I know who this Mrs. Byrd is now," said the constable, "since you've associated her with Mr. Dyer, who we know very well indeed. She was convicted with him for theft and sent down for a year. So she's coming out in October or thereabouts,they often let the women out early too. Sir, excuse my asking, but how did a gentleman get to be into - that sorry state you're in? Just curious."

"I angered my father, and he believed it would be good for me to live on my wits for a year. He believes in toughening a man up. But I can't find a position because I have no references, so I'm in a doss-house, and lucky not to be eaten alive."

"And – if you don't mind my asking, is it working, sir? You're father's scheme?"

Ethan smiled ruefully.

"I have seen a side of life I did not know existed. My father may find me more grateful than heretofore. I don't suppose you have seen a young woman, a beautiful young woman, with an infant, hereabouts? Well-dressed? A lady?"

He gave them Daphne's name, a brief description, and showed them her photograph. They shook their heads. When he was about to leave, the constable said:

"Well sir, if you're down on your luck, and if you don't mind my giving you a piece of advice, get out to the country and help with the harvests. They're always looking for hands."

CHAPTER SEVENTY-ONE

E than took the policeman's advice and the following day began a trek out to the country, in the direction of York. He tried three farms without luck, but the third farmer directed him to Redmond's, who generally took on many farmhands at this time of year. Even Redmond was reluctant until Ethan said he only required board and lodging. Farmer Redmond was impressed, and told him he couldn't have him work for nothing and they settled on five shillings a week. He was shown to the stables, where he espied a tin bath, rough soap, a piece of flannel and a none-too-clean towel. He filled the bath with cold water from a tap and had his first bath in weeks.

The following morning, Ethan embarked on what he would remember later in life as the most fulfilling time of his life to that date. This spoiled, petulant young man rose from his bed of straw in the stables at dawn, washed under the tap in the yard, and after a cup of water and a slice of bread in the farmhouse kitchen, went out to work in the fields with a scythe. At nine o'clock, he and the other hands came into the kitchen for a breakfast of eggs, bacon and fried bread. Again, to the scythe. Half-past twelve saw the hungry men eat a hearty dinner. They worked all the afternoon with just a short break for water at half-past three, and at six o'clock supper was served. Only he and two others slept on the farm, as the others' homes were local. He became friends with them, though Ned and Will were wary first of this man who was not of their class, and who needed time to get used to the scythe, the sickle and the other farm implements. But Ethan was determined to work hard, and set himself to his tasks, and though he occasioned a little sarcastic humour because of his not knowing how to do this or that, he endured it also with humour, which caused them to like him instead of looking down upon him. The first week was very hard indeed, sore muscles plagued him, and his back felt as if it was going to break. But his body adapted to these new demands quickly.

Ethan felt better than he had ever felt in his life. The hard work energised him rather than tired him. His mood became more optimistic, his heart less burdened. He saw a Power greater than he in the works of nature around him, and felt humbled. He grew to love the animals, the fields, the streams, the little stone church everybody attended on Sundays, the jovial farmer and his hardworking, sensible wife. They were a happy couple, each sure of the other's role, a great team. He wanted to be as happy as Farmer Redmond. Daphne was never out of his thoughts.

He knew Mrs. Redmond was very curious about him. One Saturday evening, when the other lads had gone to a dance, she invited him to sit with them in the farmhouse kitchen, and asked him:

"Now Ethan, you mun tell us about yerself. We need a good story, Freddie and me. Come on, now!" She was knitting by the fire, the needles clicking busily.

He gave in to her coaxing, and told them frankly what had happened to him without a shred of self-pity – the forced marriage, how he had neglected his wife, how he had been very ungrateful that she had given him only a daughter.

"I was mentally cruel. I admit it freely."

"An' she loved you. You broke 'er heart."

"You think very badly of me now." he said, wringing his hands, looking at the stone flags.

"Not if you 'ave learned. But let me give you a word of advice, Ethan." said Mrs. Redmond, warming to the subject. "When you do find 'er, court her. Court her properly, as if you wasn't ever married. There's a lot of people that 'ave to learn, about how to be good to their wives or husbands, and many of 'em – not all, mind you, step up to it. Like your Uncle Edward, husband, who nearly drank the farm, and broke his wife's heart, before he come to his senses. Well now, Ethan, that was a great story you told, and it passed the night for us. You mun write and tell us how it ended, promise? Now for a cuppa tea." The clicking ceased and she put down her knitting, satisfied.

After the six weeks was done, he took his bag and a good reference and waved goodbye to Farmer Redmond and his wife, and travelled to York on a succession of carts going in that direction. He had some money now, but wanted to save as much as he could, for he did not know what he would do in York, except to contact Daphne's mother. He wished to warn her about Dyer.

He hoped very much that Mrs. Byrd knew something of Daphne.

York, a quaint city which retained many of its medieval features, was like no other city that Ethan had ever been. At another time he might have been very interested in exploring its fine Roman walls, narrow cobbled streets, Tudor buildings, and the famous Minster, the church to which all streets seemed to lead. But Ethan had one aim – to find Mrs. Byrd.

The women's prison at York Castle had a grand imposing front, like a palace, as if hiding the cold stone cells and the miserable souls confined within.

To his dismay, he learned that Mrs. Byrd had been released only the day before.

"Where did she go to?" he asked the matron, in an agitated manner.

"I don't know. She had a daughter come visit her recently, so maybe she went to her."

Ethan's heart soared. Daphne, it must be Daphne! Please God let it be Daphne! She'd found out her mother was in prison and had come to her!

CHAPTER SEVENTY-TWO

Daphne was posing as a widow, and in her heart, she felt like one. She had come straight to York to be near Becky. The two sisters were overjoyed to be together again, and Becky loved her little niece, a plump, smiling baby, though she was the image of her father, that loathsome fellow Webster. Becky had no hesitation now in telling Daffy all about their mother's misfortune, and Daphne was very distressed indeed. She only thanked God that the news of her mother's crime had not reached Victoria Park, as this would have been another reason for her in-laws to have made her miserable. It might even have turned her father-in-law against her!

She knew her money would eventually run out, so Becky asked her mistress for help in finding her some employment. Daphne was a talented seamstress, and sewing was something she could do at home while minding her baby. She took a small upstairs flat near Becky, cheap but clean, and sent the address to her mother. As Mrs. Byrd had used up her allotment of visitors, she had not been able to see her but eagerly awaited the knock on the door sometime in

October. Her front window looked out on the street, and as she often sewed by the window for the light, she had a habit of looking up and out to see comings and goings.

Every day she felt free, so free, of the Websters. She'd shaken them off as if they were so many biting ants on her back and she did not care if she never saw any of them again. She wondered how Ethan reacted to her letter. He had probably cursed and thrown it into the fire.

The entire marriage had been a shambles. Except for her beautiful Emmy of course!

She was sewing a piece of lace onto a bodice one morning, and looked up to see a familiar female figure, shawled and slightly bowed, advance down the street. Her heart did a little leap. Was it – was it – her Mamma? The woman was consulting a piece of paper in her hand, and looking at the numbers on the houses. She looked upwards and Daphne jumped up with joy.

CHAPTER SEVENTY-THREE

E than decided that instead of looking for Daphne or her mother, much as he wished to, he must first look for somebody else – the man Dyer, or Montague. He'd find him and tip off the police, so that he could be locked up again without doing any harm to his mother-in-law.

Where was such a man likely to be? His world was the illegal gambling houses, the taverns, the doss-houses where he could find accomplices, desperate people who needed his protection.

"I'm lookin' for a bit of night life and fun," he said to the landlord of a pub he visited for a bite to eat. "But I'm new 'ere, and don't know where I'd go to find it."

The landlord knew only too well what he meant, and he was directed to the streets around Grape Lane and Petersgate.

"I'm searchin' for an old friend," he said to the landlord of the third place he tried, a raucous pub with a band playing. "I need ter find him. His name is Montague, and he likes a flutter. Also known as Dyer."

"I don't want trouble 'ere. I haven't seen you 'ere afore now, for all I know you are an undercover, but they dress a good bit better'n you do, an' wash theirselves. Make it worth my while, and you might be lucky."

Ethan laughed. He took eight half-crowns from his pocket and jingled them.

"E'll be in later," said the landlord. The money changed hands without anybody noticing, and Ethan drank a quart of beer in sight of the door before the landlord caught his eye as a thin man, with a cap pulled down over his eyes came in and joined a group of other men in the corner. Ethan glanced at him. He was well-dressed and had a cane.

Ethan's intention had been to get up and find a policeman, but now he was uneasy about allowing the man out of his sight. What was to stop the landlord mentioning that somebody had been enquiring for him? He decided to stay until Dyer left, which was about two hours later.

He followed him quietly through several narrow, winding streets until he finally stopped before a house and let himself in the doorway with a key. A light was lit upstairs. He'd wait until the light went out again to go to find a constable. He settled down to wait, but it did not go out for an hour. Had Dyer gone to sleep then? It was time to go for the police. But suddenly the door opened. Ethan dropped his head in the attitude of a sleeping drunk, but with an eye half-open, he saw Dyer go down the street and turn the corner. He was on his feet and after him in a flash. Staying in the shadows, he followed him quietly.

CHAPTER SEVENTY-FOUR

D aphne stirred uneasily. Was it her imagination, or
had she heard a noise, like glass breaking? She
started up. Was it this house, or the next? Was that
a step on the stairs? A burglar? Why would a burglar want to
break in here? There was nothing of value in any house on
this street. Nobody was rich here. But there was a creaking
step and now she was certain. In another moment, she heard
the door to the living-room being broken down and
footsteps advance toward the bedroom.

"Mother! Mother, there's someone here!" she cried, jumping
out of bed, running to the door to push her full weight
against it. The baby woke and cried. Mrs. Byrd, awake now,
got up immediately. Daphne was not strong enough to keep
the door shut, and a menacing figure pushed her roughly out
of the way. A man, thin, carrying a lantern.

"Where is she?" a voice growled. Daphne saw the glimmer of
steel in his hand.

"Dick! Dick! It can't be! You can't be out!" her mother
screamed.

"I am out, Amelia! You snitched on me!"

"Mother, he has a knife! Get under the bed!" cried Daphne, as she snatched up Emmy and retreated to the open door. She jumped. In the darkness, she'd run into another figure, tall, uncouth, smelling of beer. There was a gang!

"Don't be frightened," said a familiar voice, as two firm hands grasped her shoulders for a brief moment. "Take the baby and leave the house. I'll deal with him."

Ethan. Of course it was not Ethan! Just someone like him. But she took his direction, and ran. Shivering in her nightgown, she ran down the stairs and into the street, where a small crowd was gathering.

Ethan! So like his voice! No, she was mistaken. She shivered and trembled and her neighbour put a shawl around her shoulders, wanting to lead her inside to her home.

"Mamma!" she whispered. "Oh God, keep Mamma safe!"

There were shouts and screams from the room above, and two police constables arrived with a lantern and batons drawn.

A few more shouts, filthy curses, not fit for anybody's hearing.

Daphne was led into her neighbour's house and given a chair. Somebody stirred up the smouldering embers of the fire and placed the kettle over it. It began to sing. A gas lamp hissed.

It was her imagination, thinking that the second man was Ethan. How silly!

"Mamma! Where's Mamma?" she asked, anxiously, rocking Emmy.

"I'm here, dear." Her mother came in just then, wrapped in her shawl. Apart from shaking like a leaf, she appeared to be unhurt.

"Where's – where's – that man?"

"He's in custody. I told the police who 'e was. Oh Daffy, I had no idea 'e was out! I thought I would be safe from 'im. That other man saved me. I got under the bed, and Montague pulled me out. The other man pulled 'im off me, then I heard 'im give a loud cry, 'e must have been stabbed with the shiv. But as I was running from the room, I saw him get up, and take the chair, and went for 'im with the chair in front of him, pinning 'im against the wall."

"But who was stabbed, Mother? Who? Tell me!"

"It was the other man, the man who pulled Dick off of me. He got it deep in the stomach! He gave an awful groan, 'e said something – it sounded like your name! *'Daffy'* – afore he got up again! Who is 'e?"

"I must go to him!" Daphne cried, handing her mother the baby.

She ran outside and past the policeman at the door, saying that she needed to see the man who rescued her mother.

"We called the doctor, Ma'am. We don't know if he'll live, but go up and see 'im if you wish."

Daphne rushed up the stairs. The room was well-lit now, and it was indeed Ethan, lying on the floor, his shirt torn open, with blood everywhere. A constable leaned over him, pressing down hard on his stomach with a crumpled-up pillow cover. Ethan's eyes were shut.

"Ethan!" She felt his forehead, it was clammy. His breathing was shallow. But he opened his eyes at her voice, and she saw a little smile.

"I'm so terribly sorry, Daffy. I love you and our little girl. Please, darling?" His voice was so weak, so unlike himself, that she burst into tears. He raised his hand, a chilly hand, to her face. His eyes appeared to glaze over and he shut them again.

"Oh Ethan, darling, please live! You must fight!"

"Out of the way, please." said a man, roughly pushing her aside. "Bring the light near!" The doctor got to his knees and straight to work.

CHAPTER SEVENTY-FIVE

It was been touch and go. Ethan lost a great deal of blood, but the wound had touched no vital organ, barely missing the aorta. The doctor had stitched him up, and sent a nurse who had dealt with many wounds like this in the Crimean War. She came every day. Ethan was in a great deal of pain, but he felt peaceful and was sure he would recover in time.

Daphne and her mother nursed him with devotion and care. The doctor prescribed boiled liver, boiled chicken and bone marrow broth on a daily basis. Ethan disliked the bone marrow but drank it daily.

Mr. Webster visited as soon as he was notified by Daphne, and laid out a great deal of money for his son's care. He moved the entire family to a good house of his choosing, outside the city, with better ventilation and a staff of servants.

Becky came as soon as she heard about the incident, and wrote Mr. Fountain and his mother a detailed account. Mrs.

Havershall came all the way to visit, bearing various cordials and cures, few of which were approved by the doctor, to her chagrin. She had, however, a position for Mrs. Byrd, should she like to take it. A man and his wife, who lived simply and never kept any alcohol in the house. In former years, he had been over-fond of it, resulting in deep unhappiness for both of them. He too had stolen to keep his habit, and had served time in prison. They would welcome her into their home as housekeeper.

One morning shortly after breakfast, the manservant announced "Mrs. Corbett and Miss Webster." Daphne's heart did a little twist. She did not want to see them, but Ethan was their brother, and they were fond of him. She supposed that they'd blame her for this also, or blame her mother, more likely.

She received them coolly and showed them upstairs. They broke down at the sight of their brother. Daphne's heart melted. They stayed to lunch and everybody was cordial. Helena lavished attention on Emmy. Lavinia was expecting a child, and she took a mild interest. She seemed to have mellowed a little. Perhaps life with her in-laws had taught her a few lessons. Perhaps time would heal the wounds. Daphne still did not trust her, but no longer feared her. They would never have to live under the same roof again.

Daphne had found the letter she had written Ethan in the pocket of the shirt he had been wearing on the night he was stabbed. So he had not thrown it away, but kept it close. It told her many things that Ethan did not need to tell her. It was grubby, dog-eared and heavily stained with his blood. She burned it.

As soon as Ethan was well enough to sit up in bed, Daphne placed his daughter beside him. She delighted him with her smiles, and he learned how much a child could expand his capacity to love. One day, she babbled "Papa!" and he felt that, next to finding Daphne, that this was the happiest day of his life.

As he recovered, he remembered Mrs. Redmond's advice and courted Daphne. Flowers, bonbons, pretty gifts and even poetry came her way as Ethan made his long, slow recovery.

He began to sit out of bed, and then take walks in the pretty gardens, and after several months, began to talk of going back to Manchester.

"But I have a question to ask of you, Daphne." he said one day in the conservatory where they were taking tea. Unexpectedly, he dropped a little painfully down on one knee.

"Dear Daphne, will you do me the honour of becoming my wife?" he asked.

She was very surprised at this, but knowing what he was about, was delighted to consent. She then had to help him up.

"When will we go home?" he asked.

"Ethan, I don't wish to return to Victoria Park." she said in a low tone.

He was about to argue, for it was the Webster home, and his to inherit, but thought better of it. He was learning to listen.

"What would you like to do, Daffy?"

"Now that your father has restored everything to you, could we not live on our own? Your father still has Helena to housekeep for him, and I would so love my own little establishment."

"Of course," he said, chasing away his own wishes in the matter. "What have you in mind?"

"A little villa, with a porch, and balcony – bay windows – all white, with pink trim! On a hill overlooking the city, so Emmy can grow up in the country, all rosy-cheeked! And Becky and Jem come to visit—and Mamma!"

"I think that would be charming, Daffy. I'll send for an agent tomorrow. But before we go back, you and I are going to have a wedding journey, to Scarborough, because our first one--" he did not need to finish the sentence.

"Ethan!" Her face lit up. "I am completely happy now!"

Click here for your free copy of Whitechapel Waif
PureRead.com/victorian

Thanks again for reading.
See you soon!

LOVE VICTORIAN ROMANCE?

If you enjoyed this story why not continue straight away with other books in our PureRead Victorian Romance library?

Read them all...

Victorian Slum Girl's Dream

Poor Girl's Hope

The Lost Orphan of Cheapside

Born a Workhouse Baby

The Lowly Maid's Triumph

Poor Girl's Hope

The Victorian Millhouse Sisters

Dora's Workhouse Child

Saltwick River Orphan

Workhouse Girl and The Veiled Lady

OUR GIFT TO YOU

AS A WAY TO SAY THANK YOU WE WOULD LOVE TO SEND YOU THIS BEAUTIFUL STORY FREE OF CHARGE.

Click here for your free copy of Whitechapel Waif

PureRead.com/victorian

At PureRead we publish books you can trust. Great tales without smut or swearing, but with all of the mystery and romance you expect from a great story.

Be the first to know when we release new books, take part in our fun competitions, and get surprise free books in your inbox by signing up to our free VIP Reader list.

As a thank you you'll receive a copy of Whitechapel Waif straight away in you inbox.

Click here for your free copy of Whitechapel Waif

PureRead.com/victorian

Printed in Great Britain
by Amazon